MW01047344

THE
SKY CLOWNS

by John Tomerlin

E. P. DUTTON & CO., INC. | NEW YORK

Copyright © 1973 by John Tomerlin

All rights reserved. No part of this publication may be
reproduced or transmitted in any form or by any means,
electronic or mechanical, including photocopy, recording,
or any information storage and retrieval system now
known or to be invented, without permission in writing
from the publisher, except by a reviewer who wishes to
quote brief passages in connection with a review written
for inclusion in a magazine, newspaper, or broadcast.

Published simultaneously in Canada by Clarke,
Irwin & Company Limited, Toronto and Vancouver

SBN: 0-525-39450-8   LCC: 72-78089

Designed by Riki Levinson
Printed in the U.S.A.
First Edition

The Sky Clowns

WEST WARD SCHOOL
WABASH, IND.

Other books by John Tomerlin

The Fledgling

The Magnificent Jalopy

The Nothing Special

Prisoner of the Iroquois

$4.95

THE SKY CLOWNS

by
John Tomerlin

Was it only a few years ago that he first held the controls of a biplane, experiencing the mood and movement of the sky? Rich Newman couldn't believe how much he had learned from aerobatics ace Carlie Hatcher. And now Rich was a flying member of the Tompkins International Air Show, dazzling the crowds with chandelle, inside loop, snap roll, dive, and hammerhead stall.

But Rich knew that times were bad for Tommy Tompkins' air show. People were more interested in jet and space travel these days. Rich tried to think about a career, but he really just wanted to be the best stunt flier around. How Rich is able to solve this conflict, and also get Tommy to accept his decision, is part of an engrossing story of daredevil fliers who are also warm and understanding human beings.

Jacket design by John Mardon

For Erin

WEST WARD SCHOOL
WABASH, IND.

Chapter 1

The airplane was very small, a high-winged, single-engined ship painted sun-warm colors of red, white, and yellow. It circled lazily, not high above the ground, tilting one wing and then the other. It described two half turns, then leveled out—it seemed to hesitate a moment, a gaudy bird in search of some unlikely prey—then nosed down into a dive. White smoke began to gush from its engine.

The plane plunged toward the ground, gaining speed, its wing struts and rigging wires beginning to shriek in the wind. Suddenly, the nose of the ship came up and it soared skyward again, climbing steeply, smoke still pouring from it. Straight up it rose, slowing gradually until it seemed to hang almost motionless from its clawing propeller. Then it twisted and fell earthward, this time spinning. . . .

The pilot of the plane was a young man, tall and slimly built, with dark hair and deeply tanned features. His face was drawn now in a grimace of strain, eyes narrowed, lips pulled thin in a humorless grin of concentration. He looked out through the windshield, over the curve of engine cowling, and watched the ground whirl. He counted to himself: ". . .and a half, THREE, and a half, FOUR, and—*now*."

He jammed down on one rudder pedal and released the pressure he'd been holding on the control stick. The plane stopped spinning and began to shallow out its dive. He drew the stick back slowly and fed power to the engine, feeling himself forced down in his seat. The plane's nose lifted to the horizon, then above it, and began to climb once more.

The pilot reached to a control knob beside his left knee, closed it, and the smoke from the engine stopped. He looked back over his shoulder at the trail he'd left printed on the sky, and grinned—this time, with pleasure. "Not too bad," he murmured, thinking of what Carlie would say.

He shoved the control stick forward and all the way to one side. The little plane rolled over like a playful puppy. "It just might do," he told himself.

He banked into a turn then, and headed back toward the field.

Coleman Air Park was a flat, grayish rectangle set amid gently rolling fields of green and gold. It had one main runway, a strip of black macadam extending north and south, and a concrete taxi strip parallel to it. Though the field was small, it seemed unusually busy; flying downwind, he could see aircraft parked around the fuel pit and on aprons in front of the hangers. Others were in tie-down areas at either side of the main building, and several were waiting on the taxi strip and in the run-up area, their engines turning. It gave him a thrill of pleasure to think they'd been watching him.

He closed the throttle, and as the engine sound faded to an airy whisper, made two right-angle turns and brought the nose of the plane in line with the runway. The white-painted numerals, a large 18 at the end of the strip, grew larger. As he passed over it, he drew the control stick back slowly and was rewarded with a gentle thump as the tail wheel touched. A second later, the main gear echoed the sound more loudly and he was rolling straight ahead and slowing down.

At mid-field, he ruddered the plane right and then off the strip.

He taxied near a large set of wooden grandstands decked with colored pennants, then continued toward the fuel ramp—a wide, concrete square in front of the airport office. He braked to a stop, reached for a knob marked "mixture," and pulled it out. The engine sighed to silence. He sat for a moment, not moving, then slowly began to unfasten the complex harness of seat belts and parachute straps. For the first time since buckling himself in, he felt weak and shaky—a little frightened.

Had it been all right?

Suddenly, he was uncertain. That stall entry hadn't been as clean as he'd have liked, and now that he thought of it, he'd kicked rudder a fraction too soon, before the break. That couldn't have looked good. Well, there was one way to find out, of course. He opened the door of the plane and climbed down from it.

There were several other ships parked in the fueling area and at the edge of the concrete apron, and a number of people were moving about. A few called to him or waved as he walked across the pavement. He waved back. He was hardly aware of them; he was aware only of the two men he saw standing at the far corner of the apron. One was leaning against the cowling of a big, radial-engine biplane; the other, a man in a business suit, stood talking to him.

The man in the business suit looked up, smiled, and nodded. The other, who wore a scarred leather jacket and shapeless, grease-stained pants, turned his head slowly and gazed at the newcomer. "Back already?" he said.

"Yeah. . . . Sorry about that hammerhead."

The man in the jacket nodded. "Not too bad," he said. He studied the toes of his unpolished shoes. "In fact, it might do."

The man in the business suit laughed. "Congratulations, Rich," he said, and held out his hand. "Nice flying."

Rich accepted the handshake, feeling a lump of happiness in his throat. "Thank you, Mr. Lewis. And thanks for letting me use the plane. It's a good ship."

"My pleasure. I guess you'll be wanting it again tomorrow." He looked at the man leaning against the biplane. "That right, Carlie?"

"I guess so." Carlie permitted himself a slight smile.

His eyes flickered to Rich, then down again. "Think you can handle it?"

"I. . . ." The weakness in his legs was much worse, suddenly. "I think so."

Carlie nodded. "Right. We'll go over the ground references this evening. The FAA is real touchy about that, and so am I." He fished a set of keys from his pocket and handed them to Rich. "Take the car back, I'll be along later."

Rich accepted the keys. "I can wait for you, if you want."

"No, I've got a lot to do on the Bucher. I'll hitch a ride in with one of the fellows."

"Okay, see you later." He turned to the other man. "You too, Mr. Lewis. And thanks."

"Good luck, Richie."

He walked out to the parking lot behind the airport office to find the car. His step felt light—a floating sensation caused partly by the maneuvers he'd performed in the plane, and partly by his joy. He saw a late-model twin, a two-engine craft, coming in to land, and thought: "They're coming. Everyone's coming—"

It was as though they all were coming to see him.

He drove out of the parking lot and along the road to town. On either side spread even squares of farmland, with white-frame houses under leafy shade trees. The houses were bordered by gardens and tidy picket fences, and the peaceful countryside seemed to doze in the late-afternoon sun. Rich felt sleepy too. Elation lay quiet in him now, a safe and comfortable thing. How long had he waited for this day? All his life, it seemed. Yet it couldn't have been very long—two years before, he'd never even sat in a small plane, and had flown only in commercial liners. Two short years ago. . . .

It was then he'd moved to Kansas, to the small farm his folks had bought near the town of El Dorado. And there he'd found the little airport that nestled in a palm of land behind his father's fields. He'd met Tommy Tomkins and his daughter, Debbie; Carlie, Skip, and all the rest. He'd taken his first *real* airplane ride, one where he'd held the controls himself and experienced the mood and movement of the sky. He learned that the wind was a living thing; it had weight and substance, strength to support the burden of plane and passengers, power enough to lift them beyond the clouds. In time, he'd earned not only his pilot's license, at El Dorado Field, but he'd gained a measure of confidence in himself he'd lacked before.

Incredible that so much could have happened in two years. . . .

He saw, now, that he'd reached the city. He drove past the shabby, edge-of-town businesses to the motel where the troupe was staying; locked the car and left it in the parking lot. He walked to the main building, a pink, two-storey structure with an office and a restaurant in the front portion, and wings running back at either side. It was imitation Hollywood, a place of flaking paint and smudgy windows, of potted palms and neon signs. It was typical of the drab, dusty, plastic places he'd seen so often and spent so much time in, these past two summers—and yet to Rich it looked almost pleasant now. The paint seemed fresher, the palms more believable, and he could almost convince himself that the food in the restaurant was better than he knew it was.

He stopped at the entrance to the building and looked at a poster taped inside the dining room window. Even the poster looked different now, though he'd seen it often enough before. It was yellow with black lettering and had a color photograph in the center. It was a picture of a blunt-nosed biplane flying upside down, trailing smoke. The lettering above and below the plane read:

TOMKINS INTERNATIONAL

* A I R S H O W *

———

Famed aerobatic champion CARLIE HATCHER
in his Bucher Jungman!

Daredevil stuntman SKIP SCOTT . . .
wing walking! . . . car-to-plane transfer!

The incredible JIGGS "Amadeus von Groundloop"
WILKERSON in his trained Piper Cub!

———

. . .And featuring, for the first time, that sensational young aerobatics ace, RICHARD NEWMAN, in the Citabria Decathlon, Rich told himself.

No, the last words weren't there yet, but soon they would be. Tomorrow was only the beginning. As of tomorrow, he would be a part of it all, a flying member of the Tomkins International Air Show.

Chapter 2

Deborah Tomkins sighed and closed the magazine she'd been reading. She laid it on the wrought-iron table beside her chair, then drew her sunglasses down her nose and peered at the people around the pool. There was no one in sight who hadn't been there the last time she'd looked. She sighed again.

She recognized a number of the guests. Some were members of the show, others were regular fans. Some played in the pool or sunned themselves in lounge chairs; but most sought the shade of umbrella tables or the covered bar at the far end of the pool terrace. It was very hot.

She saw Jiggs Wilkerson at the bar with Maurice Brun, and smiled at what an unusual-looking pair they made. Jiggs was tall and very heavy. From the look of him, one would have thought he'd have trouble even getting into the tiny Piper Cub he flew—much less stunting in it. Maurice, on the other hand, was slender and dark, neatly groomed right down to his thin, brown moustache. He was a recent addition to the show, a Belgian who flew stunts in a glider. The two were talking about something—arguing, if Debbie knew them—with considerable arm-waving and brow-slapping. Though Maurice spoke little English and Jiggs no French at all, they argued constantly. Jiggs claimed it was an ideal arrangement—since they couldn't understand each other, neither could be confused by logic.

Deborah saw some other people she knew around the pool, but not the person she was looking for. Rich still wasn't back from the airfield.

She wasn't worried about him, of course. Being the daughter of a man who ran an air show, she'd lived around flying and fliers too long to permit herself to worry. She knew there were dangers, and knew people who'd been killed by them; but she tried not to think about such things. After all, there was an element of danger in anything: in taking a bath, or driving a car, or even in getting up in the morning. At least she knew that the men who flew in air shows prepared themselves well for their profession; they didn't take the hazards lightly, nor underestimate the risks. They were cautious when it paid to be, and daring only when caution itself was a danger.

Still, she wished Rich would hurry up.

She was surprised at the sense of relief she felt, a few minutes later, when she saw him coming down the steps from his room. He'd changed to swim trunks, and was carrying a towel. As he came toward her, he was suppressing a grin of excitement. "Hi, Debs," he said, dropping into the chair beside hers. "Boy, it's hot out here."

"How did it go?" she asked.

"All right," he said, trying to sound casual. "I'm flying the opener tomorrow, with Carlie."

"Oh, Richie!" She swung her legs around, sitting up and leaning across to kiss him. "That's wonderful!"

"Yeah . . . thanks," he said, looking embarrassed.

"Does Tommy know?"

"I don't think so. I just found out myself. Where is he, by the way?"

"Inside, making a phone call." She glanced toward the building, looking a little troubled. Then she looked at Rich again. "He'll be happy, though. He knew Carlie had been thinking about it."

"I guess I did too. But I wasn't sure when."

"Are you nervous?"

"Who, me?" He slumped in his chair, letting his arms fall and his head loll to one side. "Of course not."

They both laughed.

Two men came out of the main building and along the cement walk toward the pool. One was in his middle fifties, with graying hair and deep-seamed features, wearing slacks and sport shirt with a western-style string tie. The other was much younger, and wore only swim trunks; he had sandy-red hair and fair skin, and though his face and hands were sunburned, the rest of his body was very pale, almost white. The two came along the side of the pool to where Rich and Debbie were seated.

"Mind a little company?" the older man asked.

Rich looked around.

"Oh, hi, Tommy. Sure, pull up a chair. Hi, Skip."

Tommy Tomkins took a chair from an umbrella table near them and drew it closer. He sat down tiredly, his face seeming strained behind his friendly smile.

"Daddy, guess what!" Debbie said excitedly.

He looked at her and then at Rich. He sighed and rolled his eyes. "Impossible," he said, "I'd never guess." He laughed and said, "Congratulations, Rich."

"It's all right with you, isn't it?"

Tommy nodded. "If Carlie says you're ready, I'm sure you are."

"Well, I hope so," Rich said. "Thanks."

"You're really going to do it, huh?" Skip asked. He'd sat down at the edge of the pool and was dangling his legs in the water. He looked at Rich now, his carroty eyebrows raised in an expression of wry amazement. "Gee, that's great . . . I guess."

The others laughed. It was a curious fact about Skip Scott that he was willing to do just about anything with an airplane except learn to fly one. He would jump out of them from dangerously low levels, trusting completely to his parachute; would ride the top wing of Carlie's Bucher, upside down, suspended by a fragile harness; would leap from a fast-moving car to seize a rope ladder hanging from a plane, and climb up it to the cockpit—but he resisted all offers from the others in the show to teach him how to fly. He seemed to regard this as dangerous.

"What kind of stuff you going to do?" he asked.

"I'm not sure, yet," Rich said. "I'd like to try some

low-level, inverted flight—only I have trouble telling how near the ground I am. I thought you might like to ride the wing for me, Skip, and signal when I'm getting too close."

Skip blinked. He managed to look as though he were turning pale which, with his sunburned face, wasn't easy. "Say, I'd really like to do that for you, partner, but I've got this problem with my feet."

"What's wrong with them?"

"They just turned cold."

A waiter came over and Tommy ordered cold drinks for everyone. When he'd finished, he looked at Rich and said, "Seriously—what's Carlie having you do?"

"I don't really know, we haven't diagramed it yet. It won't be anything fancy, of course—chandelle, loop, aileron roll—just the things I've been practicing. We'll fly them together, in the opener."

"Good, I'll get to see it then," Tommy said. When the others looked questioningly at him, he added, "That's about all I will see tomorrow, though. I've got to pull out about noon, to drive to Columbus."

"Why?" Debbie asked. "Weren't you able to reach Lou?"

"Yes, I reached him." To the others, he explained, "Lou Jacobs, the fella that handles bookings for our show. Something's come up about a couple of the dates we had scheduled."

"Trouble?" Skip asked.

"Could be, I don't know yet. That's why I have to see Lou, to see if we can work things out." He smiled at Rich. "Anyhow, I'll get to see you fly. After that, you can take over the public address, okay?"

"Sure. But why don't you wait till this evening, and let me fly you up there? Be easier than driving."

Tommy shook his head. "No, I want you to have a good rest tonight. Anyway, I may have to stay a couple of days, and I'll need you back at the field to look after things."

"All right," Rich agreed.

"I'm coming with you," Debbie said. "You'll need someone to share the driving."

Tommy frowned, as though about to deny this —then didn't.

The waiter arrived with their drinks, Tommy signed the check, then raised his glass and said, "Cheers, everyone."

"To the new birdman," Skip Scott said, taking a sip of his drink. He put it down suddenly, staring toward the end of the pool. "My, my!" he murmured.

The others turned to look. They saw three people coming along the walk: an older man, a woman, and a girl about Debbie's age. The man was tall and wide-shouldered, powerfully made, with a squarish, hard-lined face. The woman with him was small and fine-boned, with pale skin and hair. It was obvious the girl was their daughter, for she'd inherited the best features of each: her father's strong, even proportioning, and her mother's blonde coloring and delicate features. All wore swim apparel, and the girl's brief, orange bikini more than justified Skip's interest:

"Now, there, boys and girls, is what we in the business refer to as a well-rigged fuselage."

Rich laughed, and Debbie glared at him, then at Skip. She put out her foot and shoved Skip off the side of the pool, into the water. He surfaced momentarily, said, "Good-bye," and sank again.

The new arrivals crossed at the far end of the pool area, drawing attention as they went. Several people spoke greetings. The three stopped at an umbrella table, and the man held a chair while his wife sat down. He happened to glance up and notice Tommy Tomkins; he smiled thinly and nodded.

Tommy nodded back.

"Who's that?" Rich asked.

"Jake Svanne and family," Tommy told him. "Owns Tri-Cities Airways. You've heard of him."

The name Svanne was well known in the Midwest. It was connected with several major industries—petroleum and manufacturing, as well as aviation—and appeared frequently in both the business and society columns of the newspapers. Tri-Cities was a feeder line operating throughout the midwestern states; and it was the company that had given Jake Svanne his start.

"Jocelyn," Debbie said to Rich.

"What?"

"Her name is Jocelyn. It's not polite to stare."

"Oh," he said, feeling himself redden.

Skip surfaced then, gasping for air. "I've decided not to end things, after all. There's too much to live for." He gazed toward the far end of the pool, smiling.

"And you stop too!" Debbie said, sounding as though she meant it. "They aren't exactly friends, after all."

"Now then, Debbie. . . ," Tommy said.

"Well, they aren't. That Jake Svanne is a crook."

"No." Tommy shook his head. "Only people who are jealous of his success call him that."

Debbie looked troubled, then sat back in her chair. Rich wondered what it was all about, but decided not to ask. He'd never seen her quite so upset before. No one else said anything more, and a few minutes later Jiggs Wilkerson came over to where they were sitting.

"Vot's dis I hear about der shtudent pilot?" he demanded, arching one eyebrow at Rich. He wore the look he used when playing the role of Amadeus von Groundloop. That was most of the time. "You vill fly tomorrow, jah?"

"Jah."

"Goot," Jiggs said, pulling on an imaginary pair of gloves. "Den I vill shoot you down."

Everyone laughed—except Jiggs, who shook his head and said, "You know, I've got to stop having arguments with that character, Maurice. Listening to him speak French is ruining my German accent—*n'est ce pas?*" He made a pained face, which got another laugh.

"By the way," Tommy said, "I checked with Roy, and he'd rather you didn't drop the dummy." Tommy was referring to a part of Jiggs's routine where he threw a manlike dummy from the cockpit, making it appear someone had jumped. It was one of the oldest jokes in clown-flying, but it frequently gave spectators an unpleasant jolt. "He doesn't want any of the older folks in the audience having heart failure tomorrow."

"I didn't figure he'd go for it," Jiggs said with a shrug. "Too bad. I don't know why we have to treat people like they didn't have good sense, these days. Folks used to get a real thrill out of that routine."

"Times change," Tommy said.

"Oh, well," Jiggs said. He cocked his head as though listening for something, and placed one hand on the ample bulge above his belt. "By golly, I think it's getting near dinnertime. I just received a message from my stomach."

"Long distance call?" Skip asked.

"I vill shoot *both* of you down," Jiggs said, frowning.

Tommy stood up. "Okay, let's go eat. Why don't you kids get dressed and join us?"

Rich wasn't feeling hungry, but he decided Tommy was right. He might as well eat dinner now, so he could get to bed early. Tomorrow was going to be a big day.

White line at 135, and back on the stick. Increase pressure, left stick and left rudder, nose above the horizon and passing through 90 degrees—throttle in smooth and steady, and start the roll-out—*now*. Perfect!

He turned over, punched the pillow, and closed his eyes again.

He opened them. It was no use, none at all; he'd flown that chandelle in his mind a dozen times already, perfect every time—and as soon as he shut his eyes, he would start flying it again. High-speed take-off, climb to 500 feet, nose down for the entry, and— smoke, damn it! Mustn't forget that!

No use at all; he couldn't sleep.

He got out of bed and went across to the window. He looked down on the pool from his second-storey room, at the water, black and silver with starlight trapped in its depths. It was a lonely sight, but calm and cool—inviting, in contrast to the sticky warmth of his room.

He went to the chair where he'd hung his clothes, put on pants and shirt, and went out the door.

Iron-railed steps led down to ground level. There was a border of grass between the sidewalk and the pool deck, and he crossed this, enjoying the feel of grass on his bare feet. He walked around one end of the pool and along the far side of it, intending to sit in the shadowed solitude of one of the umbrella tables. Before he reached them, his eye caught a faint, pinpoint glow of orange in the darkness. He stopped. "Oh . . . excuse me," he said.

The cigarette glowed brighter, but there was no answer.

"I didn't know anyone was here," he added, and started to turn away.

"You don't have to go," a voice said, "if you don't want to."

"Well. . . ." He moved a little closer to the lounge chairs. He could see her, then, leaning back in one of the chairs, her legs extended. She was wearing white shorts and a pale orange blouse, and her face was framed in shoulder-length blonde hair. "I don't want to bother you," he said, "if you'd rather be alone."

She laughed softly, without amusement. "I know you, don't I?"

"I don't think so," he said.

"Yes, you're Rich Newman. You're with the air show. You do the announcing, sometimes."

"That's right." He sat on the chair beside hers. "You must have seen the show before."

"A couple of times. My father likes airplanes."

Something in the way she said this sounded strange to him. "Don't you?"

"Oh, they're all right, if you have to go somewhere."

He laughed, then wondered if she'd meant it to be funny. It was hard to tell.

"Personally, I prefer jets," she went on. "Daddy has to travel a lot, and likes us to come with him, so why waste time? He's thinking of buying a Lear, next year."

She said it the way someone would mention buying a new hat. As though a Learstar Jet didn't cost three quarters of a million dollars. Rich could think of no reply.

She sighed. "Of course, that would mean more time sitting around doing nothing, after we got somewhere. I don't know." She turned her head toward him. "Why do you always have these affairs in hick towns, any-way? I should think you could do it near a real city—someplace that didn't turn into a pumpkin at sundown."

This amused him. "I know what you mean," he said. "But it's hard to get FAA approval to fly stunts near a populated area."

"Can you imagine anyone actually living in a place like this?" She stared moodily past the pool, to the almost abandoned street that ran by the motel. "I don't think I could stand that. I don't see how you stand it, week after week, the way you do. Don't you get bored?"

"No, not really. We only do a show every second or third week. The rest of the time I'm home. Then too, I like flying, and I get to do a lot of it traveling with the show." A bit shyly, he added, "Especially now that I'm in it."

"Really? What doing?"

"Team aerobatics, with Carlie."

She lighted another cigarette, and he had a brief glimpse of her face—violet eyes, smooth high brow, slender nose, and full, slightly pouting mouth—before the flame died. His throat felt dry as he went on: "Another nice thing about being with the show is the people. Carlie, Skip, Tommy, and the others. There are a lot of really nice guys in flying."

"Just guys?" she asked. "No girls?"

"Oh, sure, some of the fellows are married."

"What about Debbie Tomkins? You two must see a lot of each other."

"Well, sure," he said, wondering why he'd forgotten to include Debbie. "She's nice too."

The girl smiled then, her teeth showing white, even in the shadows. "I think it's wonderful about your being in the show, Rich. You must be awfully brave. Will you wiggle your wings at me when you go past, tomorrow?"

"Sure. The way I fly, they'll probably be wiggling anyway."

She laughed—then glanced at her watch, and said, "Oh, goodness, I've got to go." She stood up. "It was awfully nice meeting you, Richie," she said, holding her hand out to him.

"Thanks—" He was surprised at her touch, and the swift pressure of her fingers on his own. "—It was nice to meet you too."

He stood watching Jocelyn Svanne walk away.

By the time he got back to his room, he felt wider awake than before he'd left it. He undressed and lay down on the bed, knowing sleep was out of the question now. He was far too excited. Not only was he going to fly in the show for the first time, tomorrow, Jocelyn would be there watching him. She liked him, he was almost sure of it. Otherwise, why would she have been so friendly? He could hardly believe it, though; a girl like her; the most beautiful woman he'd ever met.

No, he couldn't sleep now, there were far too many things to think about. . . . Naturally, he dozed off almost immediately.

Chapter 3

Carlie Hatcher woke a few seconds before the alarm went off. He reached for the clock on the stand beside his bed, and pressed the switch before the bell could ring. Then he closed his eyes again.

A sense of urgency, or perhaps discomfort, made him open them. He had to get up. He was tangled in the bedclothes; there was a stale taste in his mouth, and his arms and back ached from having worked late, last night, on the Bucher—but he had things to do. Today was a workday. He had a show to fly.

He arose and went to the window, tilted the blinds open, and looked out to check the weather. What he saw satisfied him: clear skies, and wind westerly at about 5 to 8 knots, gusting to 10. It would be hot again—hot air was thin, meaning faster sink and quicker stalls—but nothing to cause problems.

He ordered coffee and orange juice sent to his room, then began getting dressed. He put on fresh undershirt and shorts, a pair of thick white cotton socks, then slipped a flame-resistant jumpsuit—white with red piping—over his legs and arms. Leaving the front un-zipped, he went into the bathroom.

He shaved in hot water, then rinsed the lather from his face. He searched in the mirror, checking for nicks —then paused to look at his flattish nose, pointed cheekbones, and thin, almost bloodless lips. He traced with a finger the barely visible blue line that ran from his jaw to a point just below his right ear—a souvenir of his first attempt to land a Globe Swift in a crosswind. Wonderful airplane, the Globe Swift. Except in a cross-wind. He grinned humorlessly at the stranger in the glass, then ran a comb through his hair, switched off the light and went back into the front room.

The waiter came with his order. He sat on the edge of the bed to sip his coffee and orange juice: one hot, one cold, both stirred out of concentrates, and neither with much flavor. He never ate before a show. He gazed around the cheaply furnished room in which he sat, and thought how like every other motel room it was. Difficult to tell the difference between it and the others he stayed in during the course of a year. Had he been here before? Quite possible. And even possible he'd slept in this room, in this bed, the last time he was in town. What town was this, anyway?

He couldn't remember.

For an instant he couldn't remember, and it shocked him. It was only an instant, and then the name came to him—Marysville, of course—he knew that. Power lines to the northeast, gap in the hills south—the wind trickier from that direction. He knew it well. Odd how all the towns were different—and in a way, the same.

This one had a small pond due north and a big white barn to the south. Good reference points. He'd told Rich about them, and would remind him again this morning. He hoped Rich would be all right.

Something about the kid worried him, though; he wasn't sure what. He was sound enough on all the basic stuff; a little less so on advanced maneuvers, but that was normal. What was it, then, that he sensed Rich was lacking? Commitment? Self-confidence? Maybe he was just worrying because he'd taught Rich to fly aerobatics, and so felt responsible for him. That probably was it. Hell, Rich would do okay; everything would go fine.

He drained his coffee cup and put it down, stretched, yawned, and got to his feet. He felt better now. In an hour or so he'd be in the Bucher, lifting off—climbing out and getting the feel of things—the wind on his face and under his wings, the live movements of control stick and rudder pedals and trim. He'd roll on over and have a look at the ground as it shrank away, at all those people still down there, and think how nice it was to be where he belonged again: home. He zipped up his jumpsuit, feeling happy.

Today was a workday. He had a show to fly.

Coleman Air Park, outside Marysville, had changed overnight. The day before, there had been near-vacant parking lots, empty expanses of grass, deserted refreshment booths and grandstands. Today, cars lined the road to the airport—a moving chain that folded itself into the parking areas and became a sun-glinting sea of rooftops. People in summer clothes streamed across the hangar aprons, filtered into the grandstands, fanned along the grass borders facing the main runway; pennants snapped in the morning breeze, martial music boomed over the loudspeakers, and now and again an aircraft engine cracked, coughed, and bellowed to life. . . . When it died, the air rang hollow as a bell till the crowd sounds rose to fill it again. It was air-show day.

Skip Scott drove his station wagon through a gate marked "Participants' Entrance," and along an asphalt road to the main compound, inside which were gathered the airplanes for the show. Skip pulled in beside Carlie's Bucher. "Wing-and-a-Prayer Airline Terminal," he announced. "The o-o-only way to go."

"Provided you've got to go," Carlie said.

"Provided you've—" Skip frowned at Carlie. "You know, I believe I'll wear a parachute today."

"Why?" Tommy asked. "Your act would make a big hit if you jumped without one."

"You'd make quite a splash," Rich said.

Skip winced painfully. "I'm sorry I brought the subject up."

"I am too," Debbie said. She didn't care for the rather grim humor her friends engaged in before a show. She knew it was a way of relieving tension, but it didn't relieve hers. "Let's get going, shall we?"

They climbed out of the car. Skip opened the rear end and began unloading some of their equipment;

parachutes, wing-walk harness, tool kit, and a large American flag. Rich gave a hand with these things. Carlie did a walk-around inspection of the Bucher, pausing near the rope barrier to sign some autographs for the crowd, while Debbie busied herself setting out thermoses of coffee and lemonade and nests of paper cups. Tommy leaned against the side of the car and went over notes for the day's program.

Roy Lewis, the airport manager, came across the compound to them. "Good morning, everybody. All set to start on time?"

"Morning, Roy," Tommy said. He looked at his watch, and nodded. "We'll be ready."

"Fine, fine. Got ourselves a nice day for it, haven't we?"

"Yes." Tommy looked up toward the grandstands. "We've had bigger crowds here before, though."

"Well, this isn't bad. Farmers in these parts had a poor season, and aren't coming into town as much this year. We could have done worse, actually."

"I suppose so."

Roy Lewis turned to Rich. "Guess you'll be needing these," he said, handing him a set of keys.

"Yes, sir. Thank you."

A small, yellow-and-white Super Cub with its cabin door removed came taxiing through the compound. It stopped opposite the group of people, and Jiggs Wilkerson looked out. "Ready, here?" he called.

Skip Scott had strapped a seat-pack parachute over his white coveralls. He carried a plastic crash helmet in one hand, and had the American flag—folded into a neat, square parcel—under his arm. He waved at the others, and walked to the plane. He stopped beside it and looked in at Jiggs's bulky form. "Are you sure this thing will get off the ground with both of us?"

"Oh, sure," Jiggs said. "I can probably get you up at least 30 or 40 feet."

Skip groaned, then climbed into the rear seat, and the little ship began to move.

Carlie touched Rich on the arm, and the two walked a little distance away. "The pond," Carlie said, ". . . white barn . . . bald knoll on the east."

Rich was nodding.

"Wind's toward the stands, remember. Give them two or three runway widths, the first pass. Then, if you're sure of yourself, move in closer."

"All right."

"Are you all right?"

"Yes."

"Listen to me, kid . . . if it starts to get away from you, break out of the maneuver. Hear? Don't sit there and think about it, *break out!* You're damned close to the ground, and the air's thin today. I mean it now."

"All right. Sure."

"Let's go."

Carlie turned and started toward the Bucher. Rich walked in the other direction, toward the back of the compound. He was glad Carlie hadn't asked him if he was nervous; he didn't even want to think about that. He concentrated instead on looking at the planes around him: Jiggs's tiny Piper Cub with its flimsy, fabric-skinned wings and body; Maurice Brun's glider

with its fantastically long, thin wings and slender fuselage—so graceful when it was in the air. On the ground,
it was a different being; tilted to rest on one wing,
it reminded Rich of a crippled gull.

Beyond the ropes guarding the compound was a
tie-down area, parking space for the people who'd flown
in to see the show. There were late-model Cessnas,
Pipers, Mooneys, Beeches, and Bellancas, and an
almost equal number of older Aeroncas, Luscombes,
Stinsons, and Ercoupes. Some of the latter were half
again Rich's age, but as capable and reliable as the
day they'd first taken to the air.

His hands still shook and his throat was dry. But
something in the sight of all these poised and waiting
planes—the bright colors of their fragile-strong wings
and bodies, the brave sounds their engines made when
taking off, and the ghostly whisper, murmur, flutter
of settling to the ground again—something they represented of the sheer potential for flight, the ability
to climb into the air and soar across the sky, chasing
wind and clouds and distance—all this moved him
in a deeply personal way. It made him feel as though
he were surrounded by friends.

By the time he reached the place where his own
plane waited, he wasn't nervous anymore.

He did a walk-around inspection of the small, trim
ship, unhooking the mooring chains from wings and
tail; examining hinges, braces, and control wires;
checking fuselage, tires, brakes, and propeller blades.
Only then did he open the cabin door and get in.

A moment after that, three rockets soared up from the infield, rising on columns of colored smoke, and exploded in starbursts of red, white, and blue.

It was a signal for the show to begin.

The Lycoming engine fired immediately, and ran. Through the shimmer of propeller, Rich could see Carlie's plane pulling out to the center of the compound, then turning toward the runway. Rich released brake pressure and advanced the throttle a quarter of an inch. The Citabria began to roll.

It rolled into position behind the Bucher, and the two planes moved single file out onto the runway. They swung right to taxi in front of the grandstands. As Tommy Tomkins introduced the pilots on the loudspeaker system, each wagged the rudder of his plane for the crowd—then rolled on by. At the end of the runway, they pivoted to face south again.

They went through engine run-ups and flight checks, then the red, white, and yellow Citabria pointed its nose along the center stripe, cleared its throat with a bellow of power, and lunged ahead. Seconds later it was airborne.

Rich held light, forward pressure on the control stick until he had the speed he wanted, then moved it back almost into his lap. The Citabria rose in front of the stands as though climbing a ladder. Pale blue sky filled the windshield in front of Rich; only his view of the horizon out the side windows allowed him to keep the wings level. With the propeller chewing off nearly fifty slices of air per second, dragging the Citabria up through 200 feet, then 300, there was nothing much for Rich to do but sit and wait.

Waiting, he had time for a quick look around. To the right and higher up, Skip Scott's jump plane was circling lazily, waiting. Back, and lower down, he could see the Bucher swinging off to the west, starting to climb away in the opposite direction. Curiously, Rich was looking down on the bottoms of the Bucher's wings, a checkerboard design. Part of Carlie's routine was to roll inverted almost the instant he left the ground.

When he looked back at his instruments, he was startled to see he'd reached 500 feet already. The little plane climbed like an elevator! He reduced power, shoved the stick forward, and began counting the seconds for Carlie to get into position . . . eight . . . nine . . . and—

Back on the stick smoothly, gently, feeding in right aileron and rudder. The plane climbs and turns, losing speed all through the maneuver; at 90 degrees of turn, the throttle comes in smoothly all the way, the climb continuing—so that, after a full, 180-degree change of direction, the aircraft is hanging in the air, just under stall speed. From the ground, it appears almost motionless.

In fact, he was still climbing, boring his way up through 600 feet, then 700. North of the field the Bucher did the same. They reached opposite ends of the runway at almost the same instant; then the nose of each ship dropped, and they began to dive.

For Rich, time disappeared entirely. It was replaced by a series of sensations, impressions that had order but no duration. He was plunging down, engine screaming, windshield and fuselage vibrating furiously. The runway on his right was the correct distance away, and the infield was springing up to meet him, swelling like a balloon, and Carlie was coming at what seemed an incredible speed. He'd reduced power but was still gaining speed, and when he began pulling back on the control stick, it felt as though a giant had hold of the other end. With his left hand, he reached down and pulled the lever that started smoke streaming from his engine.

He kept hauling back on the stick, increasing pressure on the right rudder pedal—and now the giant used his other hand to drive Rich down into his seat. The nose of the plane fought its way up through three times the weight of gravity to reach the horizon. It passed above it and kept rising.

At full throttle again the little ship no longer screamed; it groaned. Rich waited for the slight dimming of his vision to pass, for blood to return to his head, then drew back even harder on the control stick, and turned the world upside down.

He went over the top of the loop, eased back on the throttle, and began to counter with left rudder. The horizon appeared from the top of his windshield, sliding down and under. The airfield itself followed. Once more the howl of wind rose, and speed rattled the fabric and braces of his plane; he fought gravity again at the bottom of the loop, and as he pulled out of it, a wisp of smoke flickered through his prop. A little bump of disturbed air told him he'd flown the loop well, returning to where he'd begun it.

On his right and slightly lower lay the white ring that Carlie had traced. Rich knew that somewhere above them Skip would be leaving the jump plane, plummeting down, his chute just opening, the American flag unfurling. From below, he would seem to be jumping through the two smoke rings—just as Carlie had planned.

Rich checked his airspeed, increasing it a little, and kicked the Citabria into a roll to the right. When the wings came level, he checked his motion with opposite aileron, and then rolled back to his left. This was his final flourish, and when it was done he shut off the smoke from the engine, reduced power, and turned away toward the east, his performance ended.

He flew in a wide circle, losing altitude gradually while lining up for the end of the runway. He felt tired, now. He changed hands on the control stick to wipe his right palm on his pants, surprised to find he'd been sweating heavily. Short of the runway he chopped power, adjusted trim, and watched the pavement rise to meet him.

A moment later, the wheels thumped down.

It was all over, and he was curiously dissatisfied. It should have lasted longer. Above him, Carlie had gone into a complex series of maneuvers, and because the crowd was watching Carlie, there was no applause as Rich taxied in.

He felt almost lonely, turning into the compound.

Chapter 4

Not everyone, it happened, was watching Carlie. When Rich pulled in at his tie-down spot, he found Debbie waiting. She flashed her palm in greeting, then went around attaching the mooring chains while Rich shut down the engine and made his cockpit check. By the time he'd finished, she'd come back to the door to meet him. "Well," she said, hands on hips, "how was it?"

He grinned. "That's what I'm supposed to ask you."

"Pretty good chandelle," she said. The chandelle was the steeply climbing turn he'd performed near the beginning. "I was a little worried about that loop, though. Weren't you slow over the top?"

"A little," he admitted. In fact, there'd been a split second when he'd thought he might not make it, that he might stall and have to attempt a roll-out. Everything had happened so quickly, though, and there'd been so much to concentrate on after, that he'd almost forgotten the moment.

"It wasn't really noticeable," she told him. "And everything else looked perfect."

"Thanks, Debs." He respected her opinion. She wouldn't lie to make him feel good.

"Hello, there!" someone said.

For an instant, he didn't recognize her. Then he did. "Oh. . . . Hi, Jocelyn."

"You were marvelous, Richie, simply perfect. I just had to come over and tell you—do you mind?"

"No, of course not. I . . . I'm glad you did. Do you know Debbie? Debbie Tomkins, this is—"

"We've met," Debbie said.

Jocelyn smiled. "Wasn't he simply marvelous?"

"I just didn't know you two had . . . ," Debbie said, gazing at Rich.

"Well, we. . . ."

"We ran into each other last night," Jocelyn explained. "Out by the pool." She blinked, looking first at Rich, then at Debbie. "It's all right, isn't it? I mean, offering my congratulations? I didn't intend to butt in on anything."

"Sure," Debbie said, "—congratulate away." She turned and began to walk off in the opposite direction.

"Hey!" Rich said. "Hey, come on now!" But the girl didn't look back.

"Guess I should have waited until you were alone," Jocelyn said.

"Huh?"

"I don't think she likes me very much."

Rich shook his head, confused. "I don't get it. Why not?"

Jocelyn shrugged one shoulder. "I'm not entirely sure. We had a couple of classes together, last year;

but we seem to travel in different circles. And then, of course, Daddy and Mr. Tomkins don't get along."

"I've heard. What's that all about?"

"Oh, I don't know, something to do with business. They were partners once, apparently."

"They were?"

"Years and years ago. When they broke up, there were some hard feelings. Daddy can be very sweet, actually, but I suppose he's more difficult when it comes to business."

They'd begun walking toward the front of the compound. Rich was troubled by what Jocelyn had told him; he cared deeply for Tommy, and owed the man more than he ever could repay. He didn't want to be disloyal—but could liking Jake Svanne's daughter be called that? He didn't see how; though it was clear Debbie did. That angered him, actually. It was so unfair. "Listen," he said abruptly, "—do you have any plans for this evening? After the show, I mean. Would you like to have dinner?"

She stopped walking. "Why thank you, Richie. I don't know what our schedule is, actually. There was some trouble with one of the engines on Daddy's plane coming in, so we might be going home with someone else. I'm not sure. Tell you what, though. . . ." She opened her purse and dug into it. "If you'd like to phone me after we get back home, I'll give you the number. It's not listed."

He swallowed a lump of excitement and said, "Swell."

She'd taken out a small embossed-leather date book.

She rummaged in her purse again. "Damn," she said, "I've lost the pen for this thing. Do you have something to write with?"

He didn't.

She uncapped a lipstick and scrawled the number in bold, orange strokes. "There."

"Thanks." He folded the paper and put it into his pocket. "When would be a good time?"

"Any time is fine."

"Okay." He started to say something else—but at that moment he heard Tommy calling him on the loud-speaker system:

"*–Report to the announcer's table at once, please!*"

"I've got to go, Jocelyn. I'll give you a ring the first of the week."

"Don't forget."

As if he could!

The announcer's table was located at the mid-point of the grandstands, several feet nearer the runway and elevated by a long, low platform. During aerobatics competitions, for which Coleman Air Park was a center, the table accommodated several men: judges, spotters, and timers. At the moment, only two were sitting there: Roy Lewis and Tommy Tomkins.

Tommy was wearing his "master of ceremonies" outfit. This consisted of a leather flight jacket (too warm for this weather), a red-and-white golfer's cap (a game he did not play), and, suspended from a strap around his neck, a set of binoculars he didn't need, never used, and that didn't work anyway. Tommy was a natural showman, and believed in dressing the part.

"And now, ladies and gentlemen," he said into the mike, "one of the high points of today's performances. The daring, the difficult, the death-defying . . . *car-to-plane transfer!*"

Tommy glanced at his watch, wondering what was delaying Rich. It was getting late. He had to leave soon.

"Ladies and gentlemen, may I direct your attention to the north end of the field, to that bee-you-tee-ful brand-new convertible—courtesy of Hershey Hire-a-Car, Marysville—and to the fearless, the reckless, the incomparable . . . *Skip Scott!*"

Skip, seated on the hood of the car, waved to the crowd.

Tommy wasn't looking forward to the trip he was about to make. Having to spend most of the day on the road was bad enough—his doctor would have forbidden it, probably—but the thought of what he might find at the other end was worse. If Lou Jacobs's fears were justified— Well, he just hoped they weren't.

"And moving into position—there he is! You can see him now!—our own *Carlie Hatcher!*"

The yellow-and-white Super Cub with Carlie at the controls circled in very low to the ground, and the convertible began to move.

Tommy was glad Debbie had decided to come along. Since his heart attack, he'd had little energy to spare, and he'd need her help driving. It bothered him, though, to take her away from her friends and interrupt her summer activities. It wasn't really fair, and he'd always tried to be fair. Since Dorothea died, he'd tried to be all things for Debbie—fair and just, wise and strong, father and mother and friend rolled into one. He didn't know if he'd succeeded, though judging from Deborah herself, he couldn't believe he'd done too badly. She was a fine girl (he could almost say "woman," now), and not just because he loved her.

"Hang on tight, Skip! Steady, there . . . *here he comes!*" The automobile was racing across the infield at better than 60 mph, lurching and swaying on the uneven surface. Skip clung to the top edge of its windshield. A rope ladder danced from the side of Carlie's plane as he maneuvered in close, trying to stay above the car. "*Careful, now, careful!*" Skip reached for the end of the ladder—and missed. "*Look out, there!*" Skip grabbed again and missed again, almost seeming to lose his balance. "*You're running out of room, boys! Watch it!*"

Carlie veered away suddenly, his engine roaring louder, and the convertible screeched to a halt just before reaching the fence on the far side of the infield.

"*Wow!*" Tommy shouted. "That was a close one. . . . Come on back, fellas, and give it another try."

If only he could hang on for a couple more years, he thought. That's all he asked. Afterward, it wouldn't matter, air shows were a thing of the past anyway. Not many people left who could appreciate what was fine and beautiful about a biplane. Their day was gone—his and the biplane's both—but a couple of years, just long enough for Debbie to complete her education or find some young man who'd take care of her, whichever. Two more years was all.

He'd do it somehow.

"All right, ladies and gentlemen, here we go again. . . . Better luck this time, Skip! . . . There's some wind down on the field, folks, so this may be tough. Heads up! *Here he comes!*"

Rich paused at the corner of the stands to watch the pick-up. Skip usually did it on the second try. The first miss was deliberate, of course. Not that the stunt wasn't difficult and hazardous—it was both. Riding the hood of a car over rough terrain at 60 or 70 mph, then leaping toward an erratically moving rope ladder wasn't for the timid. The slightest loss of grip or balance meant serious if not fatal consequences. But for the crowd to appreciate the amount of real skill and daring that went into the act, it had to see Skip fail at least once. Unless something actually did go wrong, he'd make it on this pass.

"—really moving this time, folks, with Carlie closing the gap. . . . Hang on there, Skipper, not too soon, make sure you've got it. Here he comes—oh-oh, *watch that wind drift*—keep her steady, Carlie! That's the way. . . . All right, now—*now!*" Skip hurled himself away from the car's fender, clawing for the fragile, swaying rope ends. Then he was swinging away from the car into empty air, his momentum carrying to one side, the airplane sinking a few feet closer to the ground with his added weight. "He's got it! *He made it!*" Tommy shouted.

The pick-up plane circled back for a low pass in front of the grandstands while Skip clambered rung-by-rung up the ladder. He hauled against his own weight and the wind's resistance, pulling himself up to the plane's fuselage and over the threshold, into the cabin. A moment later he was leaning far out again, waving at the crowd.

Rich smiled to himself, then went on down to the announcer's table. He mounted the platform and took a vacant chair between the two men. "Hi," he said to Roy Lewis.

The airport manager grinned and tapped him on the shoulder. "That was all right, Rich. Best show-opener I ever saw, in fact. For a minute I wasn't sure which was you and which was Carlie."

"Until I almost stalled in that loop, you mean," he said and laughed.

"Yeah? Didn't notice a thing."

Tommy put the microphone down on the table. "Roy's right," he said, "it was a good opener. Might even have you expand it a little, if Carlie says okay. Would you want to?"

Rich ducked his head in pleased agreement.

"I'll talk to him about it," Tommy promised. "Right now, though, I'd like you to take over for me. Call the rest of the show."

"Oh . . . sure." What with the events of the morning, he'd forgotten Tommy was leaving early.

"Everything's written down for you. Jiggs is on next. Don't be afraid to ham things up a little—let 'em know they're seeing something special."

"All right." He had another thought. "Debbie's going with you, is she?"

Tommy nodded. "Hope that doesn't spoil any plans you had."

"No, not really." He'd wanted to talk to her, see if he could smooth things over, but he guessed it could wait. In a way, he was relieved. She was pretty upset now, and it might be easier to talk later. "When do you think you'll be back?"

"About the middle of the week, I guess. If we're going to be longer, I'll phone you. You'll be heading home tonight, I imagine."

He nodded. There was no reason to stay around.

"Fine. But don't forget to call Max and have him light the field. It'll be dark by the time you get in."

"All right."

Tommy took off his flight jacket, and folded it over one arm. "If you need anything during the show, ask Roy here. He'll give you a hand."

"Good luck in Columbus," Rich said—then watched Tommy leave the platform and start back to where the car was parked.

"Looks like Jiggs is ready," Roy Lewis told him.

The clipped-wing Cub had taxied onto the runway and was making its way toward the south, weaving slightly. The plane was painted a dull shade of red, with exaggerated red-and-black "speed" stripes. In several spots, black dope had been applied in such a way as to simulate rips in the fabric, and from a distance the little ship looked quite disreputable.

Rich pulled the microphone to him, flipped the switch and said, "Ladies and gentlemen, the Tomkins International Air Show takes pride in presenting. . . . Oh—uh, Professor. The wind is from the other direction, you know."

Jiggs pivoted the little plane around and started in the other direction. With the Cub's side panels removed, its pilot was clearly visible; he was wearing a tuxedo with a coat about three sizes too small for him, and a top hat with the brim torn half away. He waved at the crowd confidently as he taxied past the stands.

"As I was saying," Rich went on. "We take great pride in presenting at this time, that great European expert. . . ."

The Cub raced back down the runway, veering unsteadily. It rose a few feet, sank to the pavement, bounced, and finally was airborne.

"That world-famous precision flier. . . ."

The plane zoomed up into a vertical climb, stalled, and fell over on its back. It dived, rolled, and pulled out about 15 feet above the ground.

"The inimitable Amadeus von Groundloop, with a highly educational demonstration of—" The Cub flew past the stands in a ludicrous crab-angle attitude. "— *safety* in small-plane flying!"

By now Jiggs appeared to have lost control completely. He could be seen inside the open cabin, struggling with the stick—taking off his hat to beat at the controls with it, seemingly furious at the airplane's refusal to obey his commands. The Cub staggered and swerved, lurched into sudden loops and stalls, fell off sickeningly on one wing or the other—and in general seemed on the verge of crashing at any moment. Rich's part in this was to pretend to shout instructions to the Professor, advice that Jiggs invariably misinterpreted or exaggerated so drastically as to invite new disaster.

Finally, when Rich suggested it might be a good idea to bring the plane in and leave the demonstration for another day, Jiggs began to signal wildly. "You *what?*" Rich demanded. "You know everything there is to know about flying—" When Jiggs nodded, the Cub's nose rose and fell also. "—except how to *land?*"

The climax of the performance came when Jiggs, threatening to solve his dilemma by jumping, climbed out onto the wing strut and buzzed the runway, controlling the ship with one hand inside the cabin.

The effect of this was so striking, the crowd seemed uncertain whether to laugh or scream. Even Rich, who'd seen the routine often, had mixed feelings about it. While he could admire Jiggs's tremendous skill, he shrank from the risks involved in stunting so close to the ground. He always felt relieved after he'd "talked" the Professor down—into a horrifying stall landing, followed by a ground loop. When Jiggs scrambled from the plane, fell flat on his face, and began kissing the ground, the crowd thundered its approval.

After that, it took everyone a while to settle down.

The final act in the show was Carlie's inverted ribbon pick-up, a demonstration of the finest kind of airmanship. This required setting up some equipment in the infield; and while it was being done, Rich took the opportunity to examine a piece of paper Roy Lewis had passed over to him. He read the note, then pressed the microphone key and said, "Your attention, please. I have a request from some folks who are here today. Will anyone with space for three passengers, returning tonight to Wichita Municipal, please report to the announcer's table?"

The hand-written message wasn't unusual—fliers in the audience often asked for rides home when their planes developed mechanical trouble.

Rich ad-libbed, "That's three seats to Wichita, folks, leaving tonight. Got some people here who need assistance, so if you're heading their direction—" He noticed the signature at the bottom of the page. "Uh . . . it would be appreciated," he concluded rather lamely.

There was no time to say more; the Bucher was turning onto the runway, ready for take-off.

"And now, ladies and gentlemen, the highlight of today's program. . . . The airplane is familiar to you . . . so is the pilot. . . . But what you're about to witness is one of the most rarely seen exhibitions in aerobatic flying." He took a breath, remembering

Tommy's instructions, and said, "You may call it amazing, ladies and gentlemen, or you may call it unbelievable. You may even call it impossible. You may be right! We call it the inverted ribbon pick-up, and we call the man who does it—twice, U.S. aerobatics champion; member of America's International Team; world-famous show performer—we call him the finest pilot alive. Ladies and gentlemen, *Mr. Carlie Hatcher!*"

The airplane darted down the runway and lifted off.

Framed against the late-afternoon sun, its slender fuselage and tapered wings glittered flame colors of orange and red. It labored up the sky like some noisy phoenix, circling slowly back to the north, then leveled out and flew on. The sound of its engine faded. A minute later it grew louder again.

The Bucher was a small plane. Distance reduced the front of its engine to a coin-sized disk and hid the leading edges of its wings entirely. Not until the plane had crossed the north boundary of the airfield and was sinking toward the ground, could the crowd see that it was flying upside down.

It came in low and flat, descending as for a very shallow landing approach, but it came over the infield instead of the runway. An instant before touchdown, it lifted its nose slightly, its engine voicing a louder and more purposeful sound—and streaked straight for the two metal poles.

There was a streamer of red crepe paper stretched between the poles; one instant it was there, the next it wasn't. In that curiously extended moment, the Bucher—traveling 90 mph, its top wing planing the air less than 20 feet from the ground, its rudder tip little more than half that distance—had arrowed the length of the infield and passed between the aluminum poles.

The men holding them ducked instinctively.

But there was no need to duck, because the Bucher had gone through cleanly, five feet to spare at either wing tip, and was arcing up into the sky again—away from the unyielding earth. And fluttering from its engine nacelle and one wing-brace wire were torn strips of red crepe paper, while Rich raised his voice above the crowd's roar, saying:

"—Thanking you all very much on behalf of the Tomkins International Air Show, and bidding you good luck . . . good-bye . . . and tail winds everywhere you fly!"

The show was over.

He stood a while longer to watch Carlie come in, ready to warn the crowd back if any of them got too near the runway. Sometimes there were a few, too eager for autographs. Behind him the stands were emptying. He was thinking hard about something, and so it was a moment before he realized someone was speaking to him.

"Sonny?" the voice said a second time.

He turned to look at the gray-haired man standing below him. "Pardon?"

"I asked you if there'd been any reply to that announcement."

Rich gave Roy Lewis a questioning look. Roy shook his head, and said, "Not yet. I guess most of the folks here today are from up north. Not too many from as far south as. . . ." He frowned and looked at Rich. "Say—you're headed back that way."

He'd been afraid of this. "Well, yes, but—"

"In the 172? And no one with you, either. Great!" He smiled at the other man. "There you go. Not a very fancy plane, and lord knows it isn't fast. It'll get you there, though."

The gray-haired man looked less than pleased by the idea. He shrugged and said, "If no one else is going that way, it'll have to do."

"Good, good," Roy Lewis said, obviously glad to have had a hand in solving the problem. He turned to Rich. "It's agreed, then. . . . Mr. Svanne and his family will ride back with you."

Chapter 5

It was dusk when the cab let Rich out at the field. Jake Svanne had asked to leave at eight o'clock, and he'd agreed. Now it was quarter till, but as he went inside the flight shack, he saw the Svannes hadn't arrived yet. Roy Lewis was at his desk and Pete, the line boy, was watching a portable television set. "Heard anything from my fares?" Rich asked, dropping his flight bag by the front counter.

"Oh, hi, Rich. No, but they'll be along."

"Okay if I bring the bird up front?"

"Sure."

He went out to the tie-down area and unhitched the Cessna. He kicked one of the wheel blocks too hard, and had to chase it and bring it back. He was annoyed—disturbed that Jake Svanne wasn't here when he should be, and even more impatient with himself for having agreed to wait.

He should have told the man to be ready to go when he was, or make other arrangements. Perhaps he should have refused to fly the Svannes, period. After all, it was Tommy's plane and Tommy might not like having it put to this use. But that was wrong, he knew; Tommy wouldn't refuse help to anyone who needed it. Not even an enemy.

The real problem was, he was glad all this had happened; he couldn't help himself. He was pleased at getting to fly Jocelyn home, at being able to do her and her family a favor, at having a chance to be near her a little longer. He supposed that was the real reason he felt guilty.

He finished his walk-around, got the tow bar out of the plane, and pulled the 172 to the front of the flight shack. When he went inside again, the wall clock showed five minutes till eight. "Still no word from them?"

Roy shook his head.

He decided to phone Max. When the airport attendant answered, Rich said, "Hi, Max, it's me. I'm still at Coleman, but I'll be leaving in a few minutes. How's your weather?"

"Not bad at the moment," Max told him. "Had some showers during the afternoon, but that's stopped now. Some scattered cumulus hanging around, bases at about 3,000 . . . wind northwest at 12 to 15 . . . shouldn't be any real problem."

"Okay, just leave the lights on for me, will you?"

"I'll keep the home fires burning. Have a good trip."

As he was hanging up a rental car pulled in at the front of the flight shack.

Four people got out of the car. He recognized the

members of the Svanne family. The fourth person, the driver, began unloading luggage from the car's trunk while Jake came up the steps to the shack.

"Ready here?" Jake asked when he spotted Rich.

"I'm afraid we won't be able to take all that baggage, Mr. Svanne."

"Sure you can. A hundred seventy-five pounds —weighed it when we flew up here. Even your kite can carry more than that."

"I'm already loaded near maximum with equipment from the show. Sorry."

Svanne considered this information a moment. "Okay, leave the show equipment and I'll have it brought down." He turned to Roy Lewis. "Store it for me, Roy. I'll have one of my people pick it up in the next day or two."

"Sure thing, Mr. Svanne. Hey, Pete," he said to the line boy, "go out and switch that cargo."

Jake Svanne looked at Rich. "That all right?"

He was none too happy with the way the matter had been handled; but he could see no point arguing. "All right," he said. "May I have your weight, please? And the ladies'."

Jake Svanne looked impatient. He gave Rich the information, though. Rich used it to calculate the airplane's load distribution and center of gravity, then checked these figures against the ones shown in the manual, making sure the ship would be in balance when they took off. The data agreed, so he put the manual back in his flight bag and said, "All right, we can take it all, if you're sure it's a hundred and seventy-five."

"It is. Now can we go?"

"Couple of minutes." He picked up the phone and dialed a number. "As soon as I file IFR."

The older man looked surprised. He turned and peered out the door. The sky was fading to twilight but was absolutely cloudless. "Instrument Flight Regulations?" he said. "Forget it. Weather couldn't be better."

Rich covered the mouthpiece with one hand. "I prefer to file when I'm flying cross-country at night. It won't take long."

Jake Svanne slapped his palms against his thighs, turning away. When at last Rich was finished and had hung up the phone, Svanne said, "You sure that's all, now?"

"I think so, yes."

"Well, fine. Maybe we can get going, then. We're going to be late enough by the time that flying brick gets us there."

Rich had picked up his bag and started for the door. Now he stopped, turning to face the man. "I beg your pardon?"

"Excuse me. . . . I meant to say, that Cessna model 172 Skyhawk." He emphasized the last syllable. "Shall we go?"

It was bad enough, he thought, that the man had kept him waiting all this time. Bad enough that he'd sidetracked Tommy's possessions, questioned Rich's decisions, and dared to show impatience. But insulting the airplane was going too far. "That . . . flying . . . brick," he said, "happens to be as good a plane as you'll ever see, Mr. Svanne. It isn't fast, you're right, it wasn't designed to be. But it is comfortable, safe, reliable—and good enough to have become the most popular four-seater ever built. I like it.

"Also, may I remind you that I'm its pilot-in-command. I decide how to load it, and how much . . . whether to file a flight plan or not . . . when it goes, where it goes, and who goes in it. Now—I'm flying IFR to Wichita, leaving in a few minutes, and you and your family are welcome to come if you like. Or not."

He had about half a second to see Jake Svanne's eyes widen slightly—looking at him as though seeing him, really, for the first time—and then he shouldered his way on out the door, and was striding toward the plane.

When he got there, he found Tommy's gear sitting on the ground and saw Pete about to close the luggage bay. "Hold it a minute," he said. He turned to see what Jake Svanne meant to do.

The man had followed him outside as far as the rental car, where the women waited, and stood looking at him now without expression. "Ladies in back all right?" he asked.

A few minutes later, the fully loaded Cessna was trundling down the runway, tilting its nose upward, and lifting into the darkness.

At first, the build-up of clouds was gradual, almost unnoticeable. No more than a faint blurring of the night horizon. Slowly, the difference between ground and sky dissolved, blended, until the occasional lights below—cars, and small towns—no longer could be seen. Only the moon and the stars shone brightly . . . they might have been mistaken for distant, upside-down cities. After a while, thin high streamers of mist began to blot out even these.

It seemed strangely silent inside the plane. Although the background noise of propeller, engine, and airstream was high, this faded from attention after a while, and became a kind of stillness. Rich yawned sleepily and changed position.

"I've got it," Jake Svanne said, meaning he wanted to take over the controls.

Rich nodded and dropped his hands onto his lap. "Hold one seven zero," he said, and watched for a minute to make sure the man was keeping the right altitude and heading. Then he let himself relax in his seat.

The words were the first Jake Svanne had spoken to him since take-off. There'd been very little conversation in the plane of any sort; a couple of questions from the back seat, just after they'd left Coleman; nothing after that. Later, when he'd glanced back, Jocelyn seemed to have gone to sleep in a corner of the rear seat. Small planes bored her, he remembered.

He scanned the instruments automatically. Everything read right. The left wing was slightly low, but Svanne corrected without being told. A competent flier, he decided.

Under cover of darkness, with only the faint, greenish glow from the instrument panel for illumination, Rich studied the older man. Svanne's head seemed square and massive, chiseled from pale-green stone. It wasn't possible to tell from his expression what Jake was thinking, or whether he was angry, but Rich decided it wasn't important. Svanne was the sort of man who'd walk over people without even pausing to clean his shoes, but Rich saw no reason for letting it happen to him. He didn't need Svanne's good will.

Jake turned his head and caught Rich looking at him. "How long you been flying, son?"

"About two years."

"How many hours?"

"A little under seven hundred."

The man pursed his lips. "You've been pretty busy. Much of that in aerobatics?"

"A couple of hundred, I guess."

"That's quite a bit. Too much, I'd say, to spend letting the blood run to your head." He smiled, and when Rich said nothing, went on: "What's the point? It's dangerous, the pay's bad, and there's no future in it. So, why bother?"

"It's what I like," Rich said, aware that this wasn't a very good answer.

"Oh, I see." Svanne glanced at him—but when the plane bumped in rough air, he returned his attention to the controls. "I suppose you've got to do your own thing, haven't you?"

It was a taunt, but Rich refused to respond to it.

The plane bounced again and dropped one wing. Svanne worked to level it, then said, "I'll give you this much, you were right about filing IFR." The motions had become almost continuous. Wisps of cloud were sweeping past the windshield. Night weather was the most hazardous for small planes; not because the storms were worse but because they were invisible. A pilot might fly into a front—an area of disturbances containing anything from mild rain to driving hailstones; from gentle turbulence to 200 mph up- and down-drafts—and never know he was in one until too late. Radio weather information was approximate, at best, and frequently outdated by the time it was received; the only reliable aids were caution, careful planning, and pilot experience.

Rich had known about the weather, having been advised by Air Traffic Control. The forecast hadn't been too bad at first, but conditions were getting worse. The ceiling was down to 1,100 feet, and Rich hoped it wouldn't get any lower in the next fifteen minutes. By then, they'd be over the airport.

The Cessna shuddered and wrenched to the left. Jake Svanne fought it, then looked at Rich. "Want to take over?"

"Hold it another minute, will you?"

He was listening to the voice on his headset saying, "—reports a front moving south by southwest of your position. Radar shows heavy rain or sleet, possible turbulence. Front estimated to arrive at Wichita in about fifteen or twenty minutes. Below-minimum conditions are expected at that time. Please advise your intentions, over."

"Control, this is two niner Juliet. Stand by." He adjusted an aviation chart across his knees and turned his flashlight on it. He pinpointed his position and that of the airport, and calculated how much time he had left, then pressed the mike switch again and said, "This is two niner Juliet. Request course change to one niner zero, magnetic, intercepting Wichita ILS at Portland Intersect. Over."

There was a pause, then the voice said, "Approved, two niner Juliet. Contact Wichita Approach Control over Portland Intersect."

"Roger, Control." He nodded to Jake Svanne, and said, "All right, I've got it."

He turned right to his new heading and reduced the throttle setting, slowing the 172 to maneuvering speed. He didn't like to slow, because they were running out of time: they were cutting across a corner of the front—one of those sudden, sometimes violent summer storms that strike the Midwest—and unless they reached the airfield before it did, they'd fly right into it. The air was rough now though, and getting rougher, and he couldn't risk overstressing the plane with high speed.

Lightning split the sky ahead and to their left. In its brief flare Rich saw several black clouds towering thousands of feet above their cruising altitude. Cumulo-nimbus, he thought, the malevolent "anvil head" formations that could dismantle a small plane as easily as plucking the wings from a fly. He switched the cabin lights full on so the next lightning flash wouldn't blind him so much.

He turned to look at the women in the back seat. Jocelyn was awake, sitting up, and peering out the side window, her eyes wide. Mrs. Svanne looked unhappy, but seemed to be taking it all right. "Tighten your seat belts," Rich told them. "It may be a little bouncy on the way down."

Jocelyn looked at him, startled. "Worse than now?"

"Maybe a little—"

A sudden gust threatened to rip the control yoke from his hands, and he turned back quickly. The variometer showed a rapid rate of sink—almost 2,000 feet per minute—followed, an instant later, by an upward surge of equal force. The motions, which in lighter turbulence tended to cancel out, no longer did so: he had to work to hold altitude and keep the wings level.

The needles on the two navigation radios were beginning to center. Rich pressed his mike switch and said, "Wichita Tower, this is Cessna seven one two niner Juliet, over Portland Intersect."

Immediately, a voice answered, "Roger, two niner Juliet, this is Wichita. You are in radar contact, seven miles west, bearing zero one zero. Continue approach."

"By the way," Jake Svanne said, leaning over and raising his voice above the howl of wind and engine, "how many of those hours were on instruments?"

"Seventy simulated, twenty actual."

Svanne nodded thoughtfully, and sat back.

Seconds after they'd begun their descent, they were enveloped in cloud—a dense, white mist that pressed against the windows like cotton wool. The buffeting from the wind was increasing. Rich risked a glance at the man next to him and saw his face still set in hard lines, expressionless, his hands folded in his lap. Beads of moisture glistened on his forehead and cheeks, though. He wondered if Jake Svanne was capable of showing any greater evidence of fear or nervousness than this, but had no time to watch and see.

Instead, he concentrated on his instruments, watching airspeed, rate of descent, and the cross-hair needles on his glide slope. Nothing but instruments mattered in this kind of weather. There was no "outside" in the thick, clammy mist that swathed them; there was no meaning to the terms "up" or "down." The violent pitching destroyed any natural sense of balance. Pilots who trusted their senses sometimes flew out of cloud banks upside down, saw city lights that they assumed were stars—and plunged straight into the ground.

He trusted the ILS, the Instrument Landing System, a thin electric beam that reached invisibly up the sky to them. It governed the needles—one for up and down, the other for side to side—that crossed the face of the glide-slope dial. Follow the needles: a drop in the horizontal one meant reduce power, a rise meant increase it; a swing to either side by the vertical one meant turn in that direction. Rich did these things —and prayed.

They were a storm-tossed metal bat, blind but not blind, sliding down an impalpable electronic pole. For a moment, the turbulence became so bad Rich despaired of staying on the beam; both needles had slipped a bit off center. He was considering signaling for a missed-approach procedure—wondering if he had time to circle back and try again—when suddenly the clouds untangled themselves, slid away, and they were looking down at the ILS landing strip of Wichita Municipal Airport.

The strip stretched in front of them—rain-black, glistening—with runway lights like silver sequins stitched along both sides. They touched down past the large, red-and-white rectangle of threshold lights, rolled along the runway with tires sizzling on wet concrete, and turned off between parallel rows of dark-blue taxiway lamps.

They taxied to the tie-down ramp, guided by a Volkswagen bus that had come out to meet them. After swinging in at the end of a line of parked planes, Rich shut down the engine, sighed, and wiped his face with one hand. "Well . . . sorry it was so rough, folks, but here we are."

Svanne was staring at him. "Twenty hours actual instrument time, huh?"

Rich nodded. "A little more now." Jake Svanne grinned suddenly, and Rich was surprised at how it altered his appearance.

"Personally," the man said, "I wouldn't trade even one of those hours for the whole two hundred you've spent flopping around in the air doing aerobatics."

Rich started to frown, thinking Svanne really was the most irritating person he'd ever met. Then he changed his mind and smiled. "At this moment, frankly, neither would I."

Chapter 6

He spent the night in Wichita at the airport motel. The Svannes had invited him to stay with them, but he'd declined. The weather turned fine in the wake of the storm, as though in token of apology, and the sky was a freshly laundered blue when he took off the next morning.

The visibility was superb. By the time the Cessna reached 3,000 feet, Rich could see the familiar outlines of El Dorado Field, twenty miles to the northeast. A few minutes later, he caught sight of a small, high-winged plane flying west of the field and tuned his radio to the air-to-air band. "This is seven one two niner Juliet, calling aircraft west of El Dorado Field. Do you read? Over."

After a moment, Carlie Hatcher's voice said, "Roger, two niner Juliet, this is four four seven. . . . That you, Rich?"

"Affirmative. I'm about ten miles south, at 3,000."

"Ah—Roger, I have you in sight now. Max said you came through late, last night. Didn't get your feathers wet, did you?"

"Yeah, a little. Had to sneak in on the ILS. No real problem, though."

"Better you than me. If there's one thing I hate, it's instrument landings. By the way, you're scheduled this morning. Dr. Runceford at nine o'clock."

"Oh, goody," Rich said, and heard a crackle either of static or laughter on his headset. The doctor was his most difficult pupil. "I'll see you later, if I'm lucky.

"Later," Carlie agreed.

He landed and taxied to the fuel pumps. After he got out, he paused to look at the plane, reaching out to touch the still-warm cowling. The ship was streaked and dirty from last night's rain, yet it looked very good to him at this moment—beautiful, really. It had brought him home a lot of times. "Give you your bath later, sweetheart," he said, and went on into the flight office.

The air inside the office was damp and musty. Rich opened the windows, poured a cup of coffee from the pot Carlie had made, then looked at the schedule book, checking the day's listings for lessons and plane rentals. It wasn't a busy day. Mondays seldom were.

In fact, there wasn't a great deal of business at El Dorado at the best of times. It was a small field, off the beaten path, with about thirty planes renting tie-down space regularly. This, plus the maintenance done on them, provided Tommy his basic income. Until two years ago he'd supplemented it by giving lessons, but a mild heart attack had put an end to his flying, and now Carlie did most of the teaching. Rich, who'd won his instructor's permit recently, also had a couple of students. Neither he nor Carlie made much at it.

It had come as a surprise, in fact, to discover how poorly flight instructors were paid. An average of five or six dollars an hour. This wouldn't have been bad for an eight-hour day, but they rarely stayed in the air more than half that. The rest of the time was spent on the ground, either because of a lack of students or in briefing the ones they did have before and after lessons. As a result, most instructors taught only in order to build up time in their flight logs, hoping to qualify for better-paying jobs in commercial aviation. Dedicated, professional instructors were rare. It amazed Rich to think that anyone who could pass a flight medical and get a student's permit could hire Carlie Hatcher to teach him to fly. It was as though a complete beginner were to buy piano lessons from Artur Rubenstein.

When he'd finished straightening up around the office, he went outside to wash and refuel the 172. Before he got far with this job, a twin-engined plane entered the pattern and circled to land. It came in smoothly, touching down just beyond the numbers and retracting its flaps at once to help it brake. It ran past where Rich stood and he was able to read the blue-and-white emblem on its tail. TCA . . . Tri-Cities Airways.

The twin checked its roll-out at the next-to-final turning point, pivoted ponderously, and came rumbling back along the taxi strip. When it reached the fuel area, it braked to a stop, its pilot waving to Rich. By the time the propellers had stopped turning, the pilot had gone back through the cabin, opened the side door, and lowered the passenger steps. "Good morning!" he called, stepping down.

"Morning," Rich said, walking nearer the plane. He recognized the King Air the Svanne family had flown in to Marysville.

The pilot was wearing neatly pressed, pale-blue slacks and a tunic jacket with the TCA insignia stitched on the pocket. "I'm looking for Mr. Tomkins," he said. "Is he around?"

"No, but maybe I can help you. Is it about the equipment from Marysville?"

"Right." The pilot looked at him more closely. "Say, you're with the show, aren't you? You're . . . ?"

"Rich Newman," he said, holding out a hand.

"Why sure. I saw you fly yesterday. It's nice to meet you, Rich. I'm Jerry Williams."

"Hi, Jerry. Let me help you with the stuff."

They unloaded the loudspeaker equipment and carried it into the flight shack. "Got time for a cup of coffee?" Rich asked when they'd finished.

Jerry looked at his watch. "Yeah, thanks. I had a pretty good tail wind on the way down, and I'm ahead of schedule. Just black is fine," he said, as Rich poured.

They sat at a table by the window, and Jerry Williams said, "You know, you people put on a good show. I really enjoyed it. Must be a lot of fun traveling around the country, making your living flying aerobatics."

"It is," Rich said. "Though I'm afraid no one makes much of a living at it."

"No?"

"Not really. Guys like Skip and Jiggs—even Carlie—have to work at other things to stay in it."

"What about you?"

"It's a little different for me. I live at home and go to school. I work here afternoons and during vacations, and take my pay in flight time, which is a good deal. I couldn't afford to fly much, otherwise."

The other nodded. "I know what you mean. It's tough getting started—unless you go in the Air Force like I did, and let them train you."

"I couldn't," Rich said, massaging one knee with his palm, "—a car accident left me with a bad leg."

"Well, you didn't miss much. In fact, you're probably ahead this way, doing something you enjoy, flying for fun. I kind of envy you."

Rich laughed. "I was just thinking I wouldn't mind having your job. It can't be too rough, building time in a nice new King Air, and getting paid for it."

Jerry shrugged. "The pay's all right. Of course, there may be easier people to work for than Jake Svanne."

"I wouldn't be surprised."

"Do you know him?"

"We met last night. I flew the family home."

"I'll be darned," Jerry said. "I was working in the hangar—little problem with one of the prop-pitch controls—and didn't see who they went with. It was you, huh? What did you think of the old man?"

"We didn't have much chance to get acquainted. Hit bad weather coming in. I don't think he's spent much instrument time, lately, in anything as small as a 172, and he seemed a little tense."

"Boy, I wish I'd seen that!" Jerry said, laughing. "Real nervous, huh?"

"He was pretty good about it. Some guys would have climbed the ceiling. Afterward, he thanked me and offered to pay for the trip."

Jerry was nodding. "He's fair, I'll say that. Fair, but tough. When you work for him, you earn every last dollar. He sees to it."

"Well, I don't plan on working for him," Rich said, then added: "Though I must say, there are some nice fringe benefits involved."

"Fringe benefits?"

"Like getting to spend time around his daughter."

"Oh," Jerry said, his smile fading, "yes."

"I got to meet her in Marysville," Rich went on, "and she's really okay. Not stuck up, the way girls like that usually are."

"Girls like what?"

"You know, good-looking, money in the family, high society and all. It affects people, sometimes. But she's as friendly and outgoing and interested in other people as anyone."

"She is?"

"Sure. She even came down during the show to tell me she liked the opener. The part I was in. It really surprised me."

"Josie is a surprising girl."

"You know her fairly well?"

"Fairly." Jerry's voice was cool. He glanced at his watch, and said, "I'd better get going."

"Thanks a lot for bringing our gear down," Rich said.

"Sure. Thanks for the coffee."

Jerry Williams left without shaking hands. As Rich watched the King Air lift off and turn away to the south, he wondered what was wrong—had he said anything to offend the man?

He didn't have long to consider the question. Carlie came in with his student, and asked Rich to refuel his stunt trainer and wipe the oil off its belly (a certain amount always spilled during inverted flight), and after that, Dr. Runceford arrived. Rich spent a rather sweaty hour in the right seat of Runceford's new Commanche (the good doctor had more money and free time than ability), and when they came in, a new student was waiting to sign up. It turned out to be a busy day, after all.

He wasn't able to phone Jocelyn until he got home that evening.

Tommy returned Friday afternoon. Rich was in the hangar changing plugs on an engine when he saw the car drive in. He decided to finish the job before going over to say hello.

He was working on White Arrow, the old Tomkins-Waco biplane that Carlie had flown before he got the Bucher. Though retired from exhibition work—a task for which it had been somewhat underpowered—it retained a classic kind of beauty, as well as considerable historic value. Tommy often spoke of selling it to a collector to raise money, but so far hadn't done it. Rich could understand why. The plane had been Tommy's for thirty years, and he couldn't bring himself to part with it.

Rich was the only one who flew it much, these days. He wasn't particularly fond of it in the air. Aside from a lack of power, its control responses were weaker than on most modern planes, and it had a short-coupled landing gear that could turn ordinary landings into sudden, high adventure. One of his earliest flights in White Arrow had ended in a vicious ground loop. Even now, he preferred not to fly her if he had to take off or land in a strong crosswind.

After replacing the spark plugs in the engine, Rich began hooking up the ignition wires. He'd just attached the last of them when the side door to the hangar opened, and Debbie came in.

"Hi," he said. "Welcome home."

She came over, and stood watching him put his tools away. She was wearing slacks and a short-sleeved blouse, both rather rumpled. It was hot out, and her cheeks were flushed while moisture dampened the roots of her chestnut-colored hair.

"How was the trip?" he asked.

"Oh, lovely. Like five hours in a steam bath." She looked at the plane. "Are you going out?"

"Not right now. I was up in her yesterday and the engine seemed a little rough, so I was checking the ignition. . . . Why, do you want a ride?"

She sighed. "Some cool air would feel awfully good—but we can't, now."

"Why not?"

"They're holding a war council, over in the office. Tommy sent me to tell you."

He wiped his hands on a grease rag, frowning thoughtfully. "Bad news?"

"Not too good. I'll let Tommy tell you about it, okay?"

"Okay." He tossed the rag on the workbench, then turned toward the door. "We can go up afterward if you want," he said.

They left the hangar together, walking toward the office. Debbie said, "Rich, there's something I've been wanting to tell you. I've been wanting to apologize for the way I acted, last weekend."

"Oh, well. . . ."

"I mean it. I don't know what was wrong with me."

"Forget it," he said. "It doesn't matter."

"Partly it's the worrying about Tommy, I guess. I wish sometimes he'd just give up the show and live on what he makes here at the field. I wouldn't even mind quitting school and taking a job—though I suppose he would."

"Give up the show?" Rich repeated, shocked.

"Oh, I know how you feel about it. He feels the same, only much more so. It's been his life so long now, that if he had to quit, it might. . . . I don't know what it would do to him."

"I don't think things will come to that," Rich said. Even the idea made him uncomfortable.

"Money is so stupid," she went on. "People can't make enough, doing what they like, and if they make enough, they don't like what they do. It's ridiculous at times."

When they reached the cement walk that led back to the house where Tommy and Debbie lived, she stopped and faced him. "Anyhow, I shouldn't have taken my mood out on you the other day. I won't again, I promise. All right?"

He nodded.

"See you later," she said, and turned down the walk.

Rich went on inside the flight office.

Tommy was seated behind the counter, leafing through the operations book, reviewing the week's business. He looked up at the sound of the door. "Well, well, come on in and sit down, Rich." The heartiness of his tone was in sharp contrast with the weariness in his face and eyes.

Carlie was at the other desk, the one used for scheduling, bookkeeping, telephoning, and so on. Rich hoisted himself onto the counter between the two men and asked, "How did things go up north?"

Tommy shrugged. "You win a few, you lose a few— the way it always goes."

"What about the shows in Michigan?"

"Those," Tommy said, pointing with one finger, "we lose." His attempt at laughter did not quite come off.

"But why? What happened?"

"The sponsor backed out on us. Too many complaints from local residents, it seems."

"Complaints? About what?"

"Oh, the usual things. Noise, danger, traffic to the

airport." He shook his head slowly. "Of course, we don't make any more noise than other planes—less, probably—and the only danger is to ourselves. There's some extra traffic—family groups and fly-in spectators —but you'd think a community would want that. People are funny."

"It's unfair," Rich said. "It's not even logical."

Carlie snorted. "When it comes to flying, who's logical? Most people still don't believe in it."

"Believe in what?"

"Flying. About half the people in this country have never been up in a plane—wouldn't go if you paid them. Commerical airlines get 90 percent of their business from about 10 percent of the population and when it comes to small planes, the statistics are even worse: less than one half of 1 percent of the people can fly. Down deep, most of the rest consider it too dangerous.

"Did you even notice," Carlie went on, "that when a small plane goes down, it's on the front page of the papers? Headline stuff. Of course, you can read about eight or ten people killed in cars the same day, but that's not news. A plane crash is. 'Look here, Martha, another of them funny little flying machines crashed . . . I tell you it's against nature . . . if God wanted man to fly he'd be born with a propeller on his nose—' "

Rich and Tommy were laughing.

"It's the truth!" Carlie insisted. "People aren't logical about flying."

Tommy said, "You may be right—but we'd better try using a little logic of our own now. I'll level with you, boys, I'm on a spot. We've got the Wichita show coming up, and it's the big one for us. Fourth of July weekend, big crowd, television coverage, and the rest. It's our best money-maker for the year. I can't afford to miss it."

"I don't understand," Rich said. "What has losing the Michigan shows got to do with that?"

"I have to post a cash bond for Wichita—guarantee the show and salaries for the performers. I was counting on the advance from the smaller shows to do it. Now that's gone. Well, I'll be dragging short final with the engine sputtering, if you know what I mean. I just might not make it."

There was a silence. Then Carlie said, "Would a couple of hundred help?"

"No." Tommy smiled. "Thanks anyway, old son, but it's going to take more than that. There's only one possibility I can see—and I'm not very happy about that one."

"What is it?"

"Cap Harmer over at Crowley has been wanting us to do a show there. I'm pretty sure he could schedule us anytime, and if the gate from that was good enough—"

Carlie had groaned, and leaned back in his chair. He had his eyes closed.

"Yeah," Tommy said, "I know. I don't like it either."

"Why?" Rich asked.

Carlie opened his eyes. "Ever been to Crowley?"

"No. Where is it?"

"Colorado," Tommy said. "A few miles out of Denver."

"What's wrong with it?"

"Oh, it's a pilot's dream—" Carlie said, "provided he eats pickles and ice cream before going to bed. . . . Six thousand feet, temperatures in the 90s, gusty winds in the afternoons. Just the place for low-level aerobatics."

Rich could understand Carlie's displeasure. Heat and high altitude meant sluggish take-offs, high stall speeds, and marginal control in maneuvers.

Tommy was nodding grimly. "We did shows there a couple of years. After the last one, I swore I'd never go back. . . . That isn't the answer, I guess."

"Who said?" Carlie straightened in his chair. "Hasn't a man got a right to complain anymore? That doesn't mean I won't do it."

"I don't think—"

"Listen," Carlie interrupted, "I'm too old to start looking for another line of work. Let's do the show. We'll fly it at an extra hundred feet to be on the safe side. The crowd won't like it, but the hell with them. We don't charge enough admission that they're entitled to see us break our necks. I say call Cap, and set things up."

"Well. . . ." Tommy still looked doubtful. "We'd have to do it next week, which doesn't give us long. I don't know if I could get Jiggs in time—even if he'd want to do it."

"Don't try," Carlie said. "I'll fly the clown act. We'll

do the whole thing ourselves, me, Skip, and Rich. It'll save money."

"How about planes?" Tommy asked. "Cap has a Cub that you can use, but I don't think there's anything for Rich."

"We've got White Arrow," Rich said.

"Thought you didn't like flying crosswinds in that bird," Carlie said.

Rich raised his eyebrows. "Hasn't a man got a right to complain anymore? That doesn't mean I won't do it."

Carlie laughed. "Okay, we'll practice some during the week. If it feels all right to you, you can take it to Crowley."

"Fine."

The back door of the office opened, and Debbie looked in. "Excuse me," she said to Tommy, "are you about ready for dinner?"

"Hungry enough to eat a horse," he told her. "Either of you fellows care to join us?"

"For horse?" Carlie asked.

Tommy's laugh showed the relief he was feeling. "Come on, we'll find out. How about you, Rich?"

"Thanks, but I'm expected home."

"See you later, then," Tommy said.

Debbie waited until the other two were gone, then she said, "Could we go for our ride tomorrow, Rich? I'm a little tired, right now."

"Tomorrow? I won't be here tomorrow. I'm going to, uh—visit some friends."

"Oh," she said.

"Maybe Sunday."

"All right. Have a nice time," she said, and went out.

He didn't leave for home immediately. He sat at the desk where Carlie had been, and examined the schedule for the weekend. He found a Cessna two-seater that hadn't been reserved, signed his name beside the plane's number, closed the book, and got up to go. The telephone rang.

"Hi, it's me," a girl's voice said. "I suppose I shouldn't be calling you there, but I wanted to know what time to pick you up tomorrow."

"How would twelve o'clock be?"

"Marvelous. I'll see you at the field at twelve."

"See you then, Jocelyn," he said.

Chapter 7

Jocelyn wheeled her tangerine-colored sportscar through massive wrought-iron gates, and sent it speeding up the long, curving drive. She angled in past the corner of a huge, two-storey mansion, and skidded to a halt in front of the four-car garage. "Here we are," she said.

Rich nodded, as dazed by the size and grandeur of the house as by the wild ride on the way over.

"Come on," she said. She led him in the side door and down a broad, high-ceilinged hall. They turned along a smaller corridor and went past glass doors that looked out onto the terrace and a swimming pool. A little farther on, she stopped, and said, "You can use this room to change. Come on out to the pool when you're finished. It's the door we just passed in the hall."

"All right," he said.

"Hurry, though, everyone's waiting for us."

He changed into his swimsuit, then went back out to the hall, feeling a little naked. He went through a glass-enclosed patio—a place with brick flooring and heavy furniture around a walk-in fireplace—then down a set of flagstone stairs to the pool deck.

The "everyone" Jocelyn had referred to turned out to be a couple of dozen young men and women swimming and sunning themselves around the pool. If any had been waiting for Rich, they gave no sign; a few glanced at him without curiosity, then went back to what they were doing. He didn't see Jocelyn anywhere, so he strolled along toward the deep end of the pool, intending to dive in. The green water looked inviting. Just as he stepped to the edge, though, he heard a voice behind him:

"Say! Your name Newman by any chance?"

He turned and saw two men and two women, all darkly tanned and wearing sunglasses, reclining in lounge chairs. One of the men had spoken, but Rich wasn't sure which. "Yes," he said, "that's me."

The smaller of the men sat up, straddling the end of his chair. He was stocky and a little heavy around the middle, but he had blond, boyishly handsome features and a brilliant, white-toothed smile. "Hi! Deke Barrett, here."

"Nice to meet you," Rich said, accepting the hand the man offered without standing.

Deke Barrett frowned slightly—as though he'd expected more reaction from Rich. "WLT-TV. . . . Special events department. . . . I'm doing your show on the Fourth."

"Oh, of course." Rich recognized Deke's face then. "I've seen your sports broadcasts on Channel 18."

"Right."

"It's nice to meet you," he said. Deke was smaller in person than he'd thought.

"Josie told me you'd be dropping by today, Richie. I figured, great! We can rap a little about some of your routines and you can fill me in. Pull up a chair."

Rich drew a chair nearer and sat down.

"First of all, you know everybody? No? Meet Don, Tina, Susu. . . . Folks, this is Richie Newman. He flies planes—right?" he said, grinning at Rich.

"Hi," he said. The others were about the same age as Deke, early- to middle-twenties. The man named Don had dark coloring, a thin moustache, and full sideburns. He looked as though he might be an actor. Tina and Susu both were very attractive—though he wasn't sure which was which—and both had on huge, dark glasses that made it impossible to tell what they were looking at. "Glad to meet all of you," Rich said.

"Give me a little background on this flying circus scene," Deke said. "What's it all about?"

Rich smiled. "A lot of different things. Stunts, precision aerobatics, clown-flying, parachute-jumping. I guess a big part of it is just seeing the old planes fly. It's pretty colorful."

"Yeah, colorful. Look, spare me the flak, huh? I've been to the movies. What I need now is the inside story, the nitty-gritty—like, why does anyone fly those old crates in the first place? A bunch of junkers with the wings about to fall off. And if you have to fly 'em, why risk your neck stunting a few feet off the ground? Get me?"

"Well, yes," he said slowly. "I think so."

Jocelyn had come down the steps, wearing her orange bikini. She stood behind the others, listening to their conversation.

"What I need is the lowdown," Deke went on. "Like, how does it feel? What goes on inside your head when you have to nosedive one of those old crates? You know what I'm talking about."

Rich crossed his arms on his knees. "I guess you mean the danger. The chances we take. What some people like to call the death wish."

"Yeah, man, that's it!"

"The feeling you get at the top of a loop, when you could stall it out and spin in. Or pulling up through a split S at four or five G's, not knowing if she'll hold together. . . ."

"Right on!" Deke Barrett said. "What do you think about, then?"

"Well . . . I can only speak for myself, of course —and I've never told anybody this before. . . . But when I'm upside down, hanging from the seat belt, trying to hold her steady—"

"Yeah?"

"I worry about my wallet. It could fall out of my pocket and get lost, see? And it's got my draft card, my driver's license, my pilot's certificate. . . ."

Deke Barrett sat up abruptly. A look of outrage spread across his face. *"Well, for Chri—"*

Jocelyn's peal of laughter cut him off. "Beautiful!" she cried, throwing her arms around Rich's shoulders.

"That was priceless, Richie!" She looked back at the television announcer and said, "Do you still think he's some hick Kansas flyboy, Deke dear?" She laughed again. "When you manage to get your foot out of your mouth, lunch is being served on the patio."

Jocelyn led Rich around the pool, introducing him to her friends. The change in their attitudes toward him was marked: the story of his encounter with Deke had circulated ahead, and everyone seemed interested in him now. They would have been anyway, he thought, simply because he was with Jocelyn.

He had lunch with her, and they went swimming together later. After that they lay in the sun and talked. Most of the other guests formed a circle around them, and Rich found himself—and his stories about show flying—the center of attention for a while.

The afternoon passed most enjoyably.

By five o'clock, the party had begun to break up. A few guests, like Rich, were staying for dinner, but the majority had left. Each had made a point of saying good-bye to Rich and telling him how they'd enjoyed meeting him, and several had suggested getting together soon. Jocelyn had been busy for some time, seeing people off or talking with other groups in her role as hostess, and Rich had begun to feel rather alone.

There were people around to talk to, but he found he had little to say to them. The topics of their conversation were horses, tennis, resort cities he'd never visited, and people he didn't know. He felt embarrassed by his ignorance of these things. When Jocelyn stopped by where he was sitting to say she was going in to change, he decided he might as well get dressed too.

Dinner wasn't to be until seven thirty. By the time he'd changed clothes, it was just after six, and Rich wasn't sure what he was supposed to do with himself. Jocelyn had disappeared, and he had no idea where to look for her. He ended up going back to the patio and sitting down where he could watch the few people still in the pool.

A few minutes had passed when he heard the door to the patio open behind him. He didn't look around, supposing it was someone returning from the dressing rooms. He was surprised when the voice of an older man said, "Here he sits in lonely splendor, aloof and eagle-eyed. . . . The young Mr. Lindbergh, I presume?"

He looked up at Jake Svanne.

"You don't object to my joining you, I hope?"

"Of course not."

Jake Svanne settled in the chair beside him. He was dressed casually in white slacks and sport shirt, had on a pair of soft, white-leather moccasins, and wore a pale-lemon ascot knotted at his throat. His mahogany-tanned skin and black hair streaked with white gave him a commanding look: a look of wealth and power. "All by yourself, eh? I should think you'd be desporting yourself with the members of the younger generation. Or aren't you enjoying the party?"

"I've been having a very nice time, thanks."

"Yes? I was afraid you might not." He looked down to the pool, where young men and women were playing in the shallow end. Copper bodies glinted wetly in the late afternoon sun—handsome figures, individually, yet strangely alike. "I was afraid some of these prime examples of modern youth might bore you."

"They don't." It was amazing how easily this man seemed able to irritate him! "Not a bit."

Svanne grinned. "By god, they do me. I can't seem to get caught up in any of the burning questions of our age. Who am I? is a question I don't lose much sleep over—the answer is much too simple."

Rich looked at him, curious.

"It seems obvious. You are exactly what you accomplish—what you do, not what you think about. Maybe it's too simple, eh?"

Rich smiled, but didn't answer.

"Yes, I thought you'd understand that," Svanne went on. "It's one of the things that first interested me about you."

"I didn't know anything did."

"There's a lot you don't know. For instance, that I used to do a little stunt-flying myself."

"You?" Rich laughed. "I thought you didn't approve of that sort of thing."

"As a way to make a living, I don't. That's why I didn't stay with it. . . . Tommy never told you about us, then?"

"Tommy? No."

"We were partners in the old days. Long, long time ago. Used to fly Jennies—buzz a town, land in some farmer's field, then sell rides to the rubes who came out to watch—five bucks a head." He chuckled and sighed. "Tommy didn't tell you that?"

"No."

"Later, there were some hard feelings. We were barnstorming the East Coast when I got a chance to go into something else—something that looked like a little more money. And was. Tommy wasn't interested, so I pulled out. Well . . . I left him high and dry in the middle of the West Virginia pinewood country, if you want to look at it that way. It couldn't be helped. I only took my share, the way I figured it, but Tommy may have figured different. He may be right, I don't know, but I guess I'd do it again."

Rich was silent a moment, thinking about all this. "It's hard to picture you as a barnstormer, Mr. Svanne," he said at last.

The man glanced at his watch. "We've still got some time before dinner . . . come on with me, I'll show you something." He led the way out of the house to the garage, where a large black Mercedes-Benz waited. He motioned to Rich to get in, and a few minutes later they were speeding south, along the interstate highway. Jake had given no hint of where they were going, and Rich decided to wait and see.

They passed the city limits, and continued several miles before swinging off onto a well-paved private road; Jake drove another half mile before slowing down, and saying, "Well, here we are." But by this time Rich knew where they were.

The place was familiar to anyone who flew an airplane in this part of the country—both because of its visibility from the sky, and because it was indicated on all aerial charts. It was the main storage and service facility for Tri-Cities Airways, in a sense Jake Svanne's own personal six-thousand-foot landing strip.

They had stopped next to one of the smaller hangars. They got out of the car, and Jake led the way around to the front, where the doors stood open. Inside were a couple of single-engine private planes, and a very pretty twin Aztec. Rich hardly noticed them, though, because there was another plane sitting on the concrete apron in front of the hangar, and after seeing it, he saw nothing else.

It was a biplane—stocky-looking with its radial engine and tube-and-fabric body and rounded rudder—painted white with a faint cast of blue. The color of summer clouds with sunlight coming through. There were darker strokes of midnight blue on its fuselage, wings, and cowling, and Rich knew at a glance what it was. A Great Lakes 2T-1A, one of the most famous show planes ever built.

A man in clean, white coveralls came out of the hangar. Jake Svanne said, "Think she'll take us around today, Claude?"

The man shrugged. "One may hope," he said with a French accent.

Jake Svanne laughed and turned to Rich. "Care to give it a try?" Seeing the look on Rich's face, he told Claude: "Call the tower, and tell them we'll be using the practice area over by the reservoir." He walked to the Great Lakes and gestured to the rear cockpit, the one from which the plane normally was flown. "This is your specialty," he said. "I'm just along for the ride."

Rich settled himself in the deep, soft cushions, and reached out to finger the controls. The airplane gave every appearance of being new, though the Great Lakes Company hadn't been in business since around 1930, he knew. He was still admiring the superb job of restoration when he heard the mechanic call, *"Coupez!"*

Jake Svanne looked back from the forward cockpit to translate. "Switch off!"

The mechanic pulled the propeller through a couple of times with the ignition off, priming the engine, then cried, *"Contact!"* Rich flipped the ignition to "on," and at the next pull the big radial boomed to life. He eased off on the throttle and waited for the engine to warm a little, then permitted the plane to roll. He taxied it toward the east end of the field.

The tower cleared them to take off immediately. Rich released his brakes and began to advance the hefty throttle knob under his left hand—and almost before he had it full in, the Great Lakes was breaking from the pavement. Its big, oddly clattersome engine hauled it steeply into the air. Rich waited for the slight mushiness of the controls that would warn him of a stall, but it never came. They kept climbing to cruise altitude.

He banked south, toward the reservoir, and checked the sky carefully for traffic. They were alone. He tested the plane's control responses by rocking the wings with the ailerons and wagging its tail with rudder. He found the sense of control so good he went ahead and put the Lakes into an aileron roll. As they came right-side-up again, Jake Svanne twisted to look back at him, grinning.

"Wonderful!" Rich cried—and the sound of his laughter was carried away in the wind stream.

He'd never flown a plane that felt this way; so much a part of himself. He hauled it up into a snap roll—a high-speed wingover—and missed his recovery, because the Lakes reacted faster than he'd expected. He set up and did it again, this time perfectly, and went directly into a series of stall maneuvers, power off and power on. Within minutes his flying had become a review of everything he'd ever learned, an almost effortless rehearsal of all his skills. He did stalls and rolls and loops, not flying the maneuvers so much as simply "thinking" them: he saw patterns inside his head, and the Great Lakes traced them on blank, blue sky. If only he'd had Corvus oil to make a smoke stream with, so everyone else could see too!

He felt so confident, he decided to try a vertical snap—a twisting, high-speed flip performed while flying straight up—which was a stunt he'd never done very well. Nor did he now. He fell out too soon, dropping into a full stall and the beginnings of a flat spin; but the difference was, it didn't frighten him this time. He merely kicked the plane into a normal spin, recovered, and began setting up to try the maneuver again. . . . Only, Jake Svanne was waving at him.

Waving, and pointing to his wristwatch, and then toward the field. With a sense of shock, Rich saw how far down the sun had slid while he'd been busy. It was hard to believe so much time had passed. . . .

When he landed the Great Lakes, he experienced his only uneasiness with the plane. He was bothered first by the difficulty in seeing over its up-tilted nose to the runway. He was forced to look out the sides for ground reference. Moreover, once the wheels came down, the Lakes was nearly as touchy at ground-handling as the Tomkins-Waco. But the wind was light, quartering from the left, and he had no real trouble guiding the marvelous biplane back to its hangar. Once there, he hoisted himself from the cockpit and climbed down, feeling a real reluctance to leave the ship.

He noticed Jake Svanne taking longer to get out. The man eased down slowly, then leaned for a moment with both hands against the wing root, looking pale under his tan. "Been a while . . . since I did that," he confessed.

"Gee, I'm sorry if—"

"No, no. I enjoyed it. Even if my stomach didn't. Uh—'fraid I'm going to have to ask you to drive going home, though. . . ."

Svanne's color improved after they'd started back. About halfway home, he chuckled and said, "Tell the truth, I've never flown her the way you just did. Back when I was barnstorming, planes weren't made for those maneuvers, and I've never got around to learning them. Never seem to have time. I enjoy taking the old bird out occasionally, and boring a few holes in the sky—but nothing fancy. I don't know, maybe I'll take a few lessons one of these days. Know anyone who gives them?"

Rich was tempted to offer his services. It would be a chance to fly the Great Lakes regularly, not to mention getting to see Jocelyn much more often than he could hope to otherwise. It was a marvelous opportunity for him. . . . Or was it?

It would mean inventing excuses to come to Wichita, once or twice a week. He couldn't tell anyone what he was doing. No; excuses wasn't the right word, the right word was lies—he might as well face that. A series of lies that would become more complex as time went by, the way lies do, and that would trip him up sooner or later. Sooner, probably, since he had little talent as a liar. He couldn't do it, he realized—and realized Jake Svanne was watching him, waiting for an answer.

"Carlie Hatcher is the best around," Rich said. "You ought to come over to El Dorado, and let him check you out."

They drove past the iron gates of the Svanne residence. Jake motioned at him to park in front of the house. When they'd stopped, he took the car keys from Rich and said, "There's something I'd like you to be thinking about. Tri-Cities is on the lookout for good people. We hire pilots, operations chiefs, executive talent—young folks who can grow with a growing company. When we find someone we like, we treat him well."

Svanne stared at Rich a moment, grinned suddenly, and got out of the car. He started up to the front of the house with Rich following, feeling confused.

The other guests were assembled in the living room, waiting: Deke Barrett, his friend Don, the two girls —Tina and Susu—and a couple Rich hadn't met. Jocelyn stood up, looking rather stormy, and demanded, "Where in the world have you been? We were. . . ." She broke off, seeing her father.

"Hope we didn't keep you waiting," he said to the guests. "Dinner ready?"

It was. Everyone began moving through to the dining room.

Jocelyn dropped back to be with Rich and whispered, "Where did you two go? Why didn't you tell me? Do you realize I—?"

"Hello, there!" said the girl Rich hadn't met before. "You're Rich Newman, aren't you? I'm Dodie Boyle. Josie told me you were coming, and I've been dying to meet you. I've seen the air show, and I think it's so exciting, and Josie says you fly in it. Do you really? That's—"

"Dinner," Jocelyn broke in, "is ready, I think." She took Rich's arm, smiling sweetly, all traces of annoyance gone. "Shall we go in?"

She was nice to him the rest of the evening.

Chapter 8

He had no chance at all, the following week, to see Jocelyn again. His days were crowded with the preparations for Crowley. Two planes had to be readied this time, instead of one: White Arrow and the Bucher. They had to be inspected thoroughly for the slightest signs of stress or wear, for fabric rot or tube corrosion, and both engines had to be serviced with new oil, plugs, filters, and a careful tuning. In addition, there was the equipment for the show to check out—banners and signs and loudspeaker parts, Carlie's ribbon pick-up gear, Skip's array of chutes and harnesses. At the same time the normal business at the field was carried on.

Rich had little time to think about anything but work. He spoke to Jocelyn on the telephone only once that week. She said she had a surprise for him, but wouldn't tell him what it was. He'd find out soon, she said.

They left for Denver late Friday afternoon. Ordinarily, Tommy insisted on an extra day in town before a performance—a chance to rest from the journey and make final checks on the equipment—but this time it wasn't possible. He and Debbie went with Skip Scott in the station wagon, carrying most of the gear. Carlie and Rich took off later, giving themselves a half hour of daylight at the other end to find the field and land.

Rich fell into position behind and to one side of the Bucher, letting Carlie navigate. When they'd reached cruise altitude, and steadied on their course west, he tuned in Wichita FSS and asked for Denver Weather. ". . . sky clear, temperature 86. Wind zero eight zero at 15, gusts to 20. Altimeter three zero niner five. . . ." He thanked Flight Service, and sat back, adjusting his dark glasses against the downward-tracking sun.

Wind 15 knots, gusting to 20? Too much for comfort if he had to land in it. What was the old joke—"It's not the fall that kills you, it's the landing"? A little too true to be funny, he decided.

As it happened, they landed in near dead-calm, dropping into a shallow pocket of hills with higher mountain peaks beyond. They spent the night in rooms Cap Harmer, the airport manager, had reserved for them, and drove back to the field Saturday morning.

Crowley Field was thirty-four hundred feet long, which was more than adequate at sea level. At this altitude, it barely sufficed. The air gets thinner the higher one goes, and the thinner the air, the faster an airplane must move to take off and land. The runway at Crowley left little margin for error even in good weather.

The early part of the day couldn't have been more pleasant, with clear skies and a soft, warm, easterly breeze. By ten o'clock it was apparent that the crowd was going to be large; the stands were half filled already, blankets stretched along the fence facing the runway, and the parking lot was running out of room. Tommy went around with an exuberant grin.

Carlie didn't; he kept glancing at the sky. By noon, the wind had risen and shifted farther east, and the thermometer in the shade of the flight shack was creeping past 80. The asphalt of the runway was getting sticky when Carlie summoned Skip and Rich to a conference under the wing of Cap Harmer's Super Cub. They went over plans.

"I'll drop a couple of streamers about twelve thirty," Carlie told Skip. "No point doing it sooner, that wind could shift again. Want to go with me or watch it down here?"

"Probably be able to figure the drift better here."

Carlie nodded and squinted toward the east. "I'd guess you'll be going out on the other side of that ridge. Should be a lot of updraft. If not, though, you might come down over there."

"I'll wear my hiking boots."

Carlie grinned. "No need. Cap says the Forestry Service chopper can come for you. Just find an open spot and spread your chute so they can see you." He turned to Rich. "See the gaps in those hills? They slice the wind to little pieces, and it's roughest just off the ground. You come down final, with the controls crossed on account of drift—and about 50 feet from touchdown, it can go all wrong on you. Here's what you do, you hold 80 till you've got the fence made, then *paste* those wheels down. And stay on that rudder—I mean *stay* on it, till you're back in the compound and tied down.

"Okay, we'll start off at 800 feet for the loop, 200 higher than usual. We'll come down to 6 for the rolls —and you can start that final hammerhead at 5. Got it?"

"Got it."

Carlie looked at his watch. "I better get started then. See you back here."

They separated to their various tasks—Carlie to drop the weighted, crepe-paper ribbons that would measure wind drift, Skip to get into his jumpsuit and harness while watching him do it. Rich made a final walk-around of White Arrow, and when he'd finished, climbed into the rear cockpit. It was early, but he felt more comfortable in the plane and a little less nervous.

He fitted on his chute harness. At 500 or 600 feet, the chute was useless; but he always wore it when practicing at high altitudes, and had come to prefer it to the seat cushion it replaced. By the time he'd connected the broad, olive-drab straps with their thick cast-aluminum buckles, Carlie had dropped the streamers. Rich watched them slant down, east to west, and go into an erratic dance just before crumpling into the ground.

The sun was hot; he was sweating, now.

He closed his eyes to rest them, and almost immediately, it seemed, Skip was slapping the cowling and yelling, "Okay, let's go! Switch off!"

Skipper pulled the prop through and called for ignition, then blue-gray smoke was spurting from the exhaust stubs and nacelle vents, whipping back in the propeller wash, shredding itself on wings and wires and struts.

Rich braced his heels on the brakes and ran the engine up, watching the temperature and oil-pressure gauges, feeling the thwarted power. White Arrow rocked gently. He realized someone was standing below him on the right side of the cockpit—it was Debbie—calling something he couldn't hear because of the engine roar. He reduced throttle, then reached over the side to meet the quick pressure of her small, firm hand. When she moved away, the prop wash glued her skirt to her legs, and it occurred to Rich that they were nice legs, as pretty as Jocelyn's. He laughed at what seemed a ridiculous thought to have at the moment.

The orange-and-red Bucher was moving, he saw, and he released the brakes on White Arrow. The two biplanes waddled out to the runway together.

In position for take-off, the wind was from the left. It gusted fitfully, and Rich held in a little left aileron to keep his wing tip from lifting. At the instant he came in with throttle, he shoved the stick full forward, muscling the tail into the air where the rudder could be effective. Even so, the nose began to track left before he could control it, and he had to apply right brake pedal to keep from swerving. He hit too much and veered to the right, toward the stands, then overcorrected the other way. Suddenly he was angled uncontrollably to the left, his brakes useless for steering as the weight lifted off the wheels. He delayed as long as he dared, with the left edge of the runway coming at him quickly—waited, actually, until the left wheel thudded on the dirt of the infield, and then hauled back on the stick and literally snatched White Arrow into the air. He lowered the nose before she could stall, and picked up the speed he needed to clear the fence. Only then did he cease cursing steadily under his breath.

Once aloft, though, he dismissed the problem of ground handling as something he wouldn't have to worry about for a while. His thoughts turned entirely to the maneuvers Carlie had diagramed for him to fly.

They began, as at Marysville, with a climbing turn into position, a shallow dive leading to a loop in front of the stands, and a roll out of this. Then both planes pulled up into snap rolls, spun half around, and came back again. They met in the center, diving, then soared up in parallel, vertical climbs that ended when they ran out of airspeed. After hanging almost motionless for an instant, full rudder started them falling sideways—away from each other—wings arcing down in the chopping movement that gave the hammerhead stall its name. A dive to reverse direction and recover flying speed, a low pass trailing smoke in front of the stands, and then the opening routine was over.

It was time to land.

Rich had to circle behind the stands to get back to the north end of the runway. By the time he was there, the Bucher already had touched down. He lined up for his final approach leg, tilting the wings against the wind, and holding the nose straight with rudder—then started down at a sharp crab angle. Everything went smoothly until he crossed the fence at the end of the runway.

Suddenly, he hit dead air—a pocket of almost total calm—and had to put on full throttle to keep from falling short. He dragged it on over the fence, chopped power again—and was belted by a side wind. The wheels hit, skidding right, and the right wing started down; when he corrected with left aileron, White Arrow began to pivot in the opposite direction. He fed in all the rudder he had, but was going too slowly by then, and the rudder couldn't stop it. He rammed full throttle on to delay the ground loop, and the rudder caught the prop blast and wrenched him back around. White Arrow skidded left, bounced, tilted right, and bounced again. Then it wallowed heavily, tremblingly, into the air.

He missed the fence at the south end of the runway by inches.

Later, it would occur to him that he could have flown on over to Denver, landed on the large field easily, and come back here at dusk. After the wind had died. Now, it did not occur to him. His panic had turned to rage. He knew he'd forgotten Carlie's instructions to make a high-speed approach; and for a thing as small as that, the Waco had tried to kill him! Very well, if that's what it took, he'd plant it hard enough this time to leave tread marks on the runway. . . .

He lined up farther out, came down final at 80 mph, flared slightly, then slapped the wheels down with forward stick. He jammed on the brakes and held them—ignoring their protest—long enough to lose flying speed. Then he reversed stick to bring the tail down with a bang. Hauling up short with further use of the brakes, he thought, *that'll* teach the damned thing—and turned off into the tie-down area, still fuming.

He unfastened his harness and got out of the Waco, ducking under the bottom wing to set the wheel chocks. Skip and Carlie were a few yards away, getting the Bucher ready for the wing-walk act, and Rich went over to them, feeling belligerent.

"Hey, that was pretty good," Skip said, grinning. "The crowd liked it. Think you could do it again, this time on purpose?"

"Why don't you just—" Rich began.

"Take it easy," Carlie interrupted. "Any landing you walk away from is a good one." He paused a moment, frowning. "All the same, if you'd rather not fly in this tomorrow, we'll—"

"I'll fly," he said, "—unless you're telling me I'm grounded."

"No."

"Then we won't discuss it, if that's all right with you."

He was ashamed of his anger, yet incapable of apologizing. He didn't even want to. He turned and went over to the grandstands to watch the rest of the show from there.

By Sunday morning, the weather had begun to change. The wind had shifted almost 180 degrees, and blew more fitfully now, if no stronger. The sky was clear except for a line of mares' tails in the northwest—long, wispy, curl-tipped strands of high-altitude cloud—the advance messengers of a storm front.

Sunday's crowd was even larger than the previous day's. Tommy watched them arrive, pausing from his preshow activities to look first at them, then anxiously up at the sky. "It'll hold," he kept assuring everyone around him. "No question about that." It had to hold. . . .

Carlie Hatcher conferred with the FAA representative, then called a meeting. "Take-offs and landings from runway three-two, today. The wind angle will be a little better, almost straight on if it doesn't change. For the opener we can fly back, and switch positions, or we can reverse the diagrams. Be easier to reverse it—if that's okay with you, Rich."

He shrugged. "Fine by me."

Carlie rubbed a fist against his chin, looked as though he was thinking of something else. Then he said, "Okay, let's go."

Rich walked to his plane, feeling curiously detached. Listless, and a bit depressed. He'd felt this way since his performance yesterday. He'd sat silently through dinner last night, gone to bed early, and wakened with none of his usual sense of show-day excitement. Even now, getting into the plane, calling on the line boy Cap Harmer had sent to prop it, he was unable to summon any emotion. The engine started, and with all instruments registering in the green, he signaled "thanks" to the boy, and taxied out.

Carlie was right, he saw, the wind was better aligned today. In spite of a couple of lusty gusts from the left, the take-off was easier. He climbed to altitude, turned back and started into the first maneuver.

It was adequate, no better; his speed control was a little off, and he seemed to see his reference points an instant later than usual, but it was all right, or nearly so. He had no strong feelings about it. He flew each maneuver as though waiting to begin the next. Flying the next, he felt that that wasn't the one, either. . . . Chandelle, inside loop, snap roll, aileron roll (those weren't it); the dive and pull-up, the vertical climb to stall, the pitch-over from the hammerhead and high-G pull-out (no, not it); and then he was flying south, cutting off his smoke stream, reducing power, and letting down. He circled wide to line up with the runway, ready to land. . . .

That was it.

He started the landing, going down with the wings crabbed left, holding throttle, watching the big white 32 on the pavement grow bigger. Too slow; he added power. The wind was strong, stronger than it had been on take-off, and it seemed to hold him almost motionless at times. The number below him made tiny, sliding, tilting movements; he couldn't correct for all of them, and didn't try. He aimed for the center of the pavement and let the quick shifts of wind cancel each other out. He maintained speed over the fence and waited for the buffeting to ease enough for him to flare out, but it never did. The wind caught White Arrow just before she touched, jerked her nose up, blasted her to a near standstill—then dropped the plane gently, almost tenderly, to the ground.

Rich taxied to the tie-down area, got out, and secured his ship. Then he leaned against its bottom wing, exhausted. It was odd to realize that all he'd really come to do today was make a landing: the one he'd just made. Suddenly, he felt much better, if a trifle sheepish. He saw the Bucher come in and went over to wait for Carlie to get out.

The other man paused, standing on the lower wing, and said, "Okay. I think you got it whipped."

Rich grinned. "Thanks. . . . I just wish I hadn't acted the way I did about it."

Carlie stepped to the ground. "Anybody can get the jitters, now and then. Forget it." He blinked at the sky, looking thoughtful. "I'm getting a few myself,

in fact." Skip came over carrying an armful of equipment, but Carlie shook his head at him. "Think we'll
hold off on the walk for a while, Skipper. See if the
wind drops any. If it does, we'll put it in near the
end. Rich, you go tell Tommy we're making the
change."

He found Tommy sitting down, resting between
acts. There were three chairs at the small table, the
other two occupied by Debbie and Cap Harmer. Rich
knelt behind Tommy.

"We're going to wait till later to try the wing walk,"
he said. "Landing with all that drag on top is tough
enough without this wind."

"Good idea. Rest of the schedule the same?"

"I guess so—unless the wind gets worse."

"Don't say that! Don't even think it!"

"Sorry." Rich knew what it would mean if they
had to refund the money for today's performance.

The Bucher was taxiing out now. Carlie was going
up for his exhibition of competition aerobatics. Tommy
made the announcement of the program change while
the Bucher did its engine run-up. The wind was carrying scraps of paper from the stands across the runway.

"Surprise!" a voice behind Rich said.

He looked back and saw Jocelyn.

"Sorry we're late, dear, but we had a *terrible* time
getting a rental car in Denver." She put her arms
around his neck. "Deke wanted to see the
show—research for next week—so Daddy had us flown
over. Oh, Mr. Tomkins—"

Tommy and Debbie both had turned to stare, first at her, then at Rich.

"Mr. Tomkins, I'd like you to meet Deke Barrett. He'll be doing the television commentary on your show at Wichita. Deke, Tommy Tomkins."

Barrett said, "Hi, how are you?"

Jocelyn went on: "And of course you already know Rich, Deke. . . . And this is Mr. Tomkins's daughter, Debbie."

"A real pleasure," the TV announcer said, eyeing Debbie with approval.

"I'm afraid I don't know this gentleman," Jocelyn said, frowning prettily at Cap Harmer.

Rich had recovered enough to introduce Cap to them. The men shook hands, and Deke Barrett said, "I'd appreciate a little of your time, Tommy, I'm trying to get some idea how we're going to cover this stuff, and—"

"It'll have to wait a while, Mr. Barrett." Carlie was taking off in the Bucher. "I'm busy at the moment."

"Sure, fine, I'll just sit and watch. Got an extra chair?"

Debbie said, "You can have mine." Deke Barrett started to protest, but she'd already got up. "I'll see you later, Dad," she said, and left the table.

Cap Harmer went to find more chairs, after Jocelyn expressed reluctance to sit in the stands. Barrett pushed in close to Tommy, and peered at his notes during Carlie's aerial exhibition. He asked questions that Tommy was too busy to answer.

Jocelyn sat beside Rich, ignoring the performance

to talk about a party that was taking place next week. Rich was invited. He listened to her, not really paying attention, thinking instead about the look he'd seen on Debbie's face. There'd been little anger, something more like shock, and after that a sort of sadness. Rich supposed she had to know, sooner or later, but was sorry to have it happen like this.

"God, it's awful out here!" Jocelyn said, gripping the scarf against a sudden, violent gust of wind. "When will it be over?"

It was almost "over" at that instant—

Carlie was coming in to land, just touching down, when the gust struck him. One second earlier and he could have added power, and gone around; a second later and he'd have had control with the brakes. The actual timing gave him no real chance—yet he fought the Bucher all down the runway with the enormous skill that was his to command.

He might have done the impossible—might have pulled it straight on nothing more than lightning instincts and incredible reflexes—but the strain proved too great for the Bucher's right wheel brake. It shot off smoke, then sparks, then let go altogether. Carlie did the only thing left for him to do: he threw the ailerons full over, catching the wind under his left wing so the plane would loop away from the stands, not toward them.

The crowd was on its feet screaming, now.

Chapter 9

Later, Rich would have no clear memory of having leaped the fence and hurled himself across the runway, into the infield. He would remember the look of the Bucher, though, crumpled on its side, and recall the voice in his head screaming, *Not yet! . . . Wait! . . . Not yet!*

Because it was fire he feared.

The safety team reached the plane ahead of him, surrounding it, their fogging equipment ready. There was no sign of flames, yet. The engine had stopped when the propeller hit the ground, and the top wing where the fuel was stored seemed intact. Rich didn't stop running, even when his breath had begun to razor his lungs and his terror half blinded him. He ran. He came close to running Carlie down.

"Hey, watch it!" Carlie caught him by the shoulders. "You'll fall and hurt yourself."

Rich stared in disbelief, then gave a gasp that was half laughter, half a sob, and managed to say, "No . . . it's not the fall . . . that gets you. . . ."

"It's the landing," Carlie said. "Yeah, I know." Then he laughed too.

The sound of the crowd had become a cheer, mixed with applause, and Carlie turned to face the stands. Looking a little grim, he took Rich's arm and walked toward the runway. Tommy Tomkins, who had managed to keep up an almost constant, reassuring chatter on the public address system, now said, "Let's have a really fine hand for Carlie, folks! Fantastic! Just fantastic, the way he handled that! . . . Now, ladies and gentlemen, we'll take a short intermission, here, to catch our breath. Why not get yourselves a nice, cold drink, and we'll be back with you in just a few minutes." He put down the microphone and hurried out to meet Carlie.

"You all right?"

"Sure. Think I'd like to sit down a minute, though. Shook me up a little."

They went back to the announcer's table, Rich supporting some of Carlie's weight. Deke Barrett and Jocelyn moved out of the way, staring at Carlie in wonder. Tommy said, "I guess we'd better call it a day—give these folks back their money and let them get started home."

"No, not yet," Carlie said.

"You're in no shape to—"

"I'm all right." He turned his face toward the wind and studied the sky. "I think we're going to get some calm air pretty quick—just before that front sets in, maybe. With luck, we could finish up. Tell you what,

have Cap's boys pull the Bucher back to the hangar.
I'm going to do the clown routine in the Cub, and
Rich and Skip can be rigging White Arrow for the
wing walk. It's a good thing we brought her, this trip."

Tommy thought for a minute. "All right. *If* the wind
drops. Otherwise, no."

Deke Barrett had been listening. He said, "You mean
you're going up *again*? For heaven's sake, why?"

Carlie barely glanced at him. "I get paid for it,"
he said.

Fifteen minutes later the wind faltered, and a heavy,
humid calm settled over the field. Forty-five minutes
after that, it began to rain—but by then the show was
almost over.

The first fat drops were falling when Carlie flew
the ribbon pick-up in White Arrow—and then Tommy
was thanking the crowd for coming, and people were
scattering to the cover of their cars. Then the rain
started to fall hard. It rained all night but was clear
the following morning, when the members of the Tomkins International Air Show left for home.

The Bucher remained behind in Cap Harmer's hangar,
its right main gear collapsed, its wing tips damaged,
and the propeller and propeller hub shattered. Later,
the decision would be made whether to attempt repairs
in Crowley, or dismantle the plane and trailer it home.
In either case, it would be weeks, perhaps months
before the Bucher flew again.

With the Wichita air show only a few days away,

Carlie had to switch back to White Arrow. He hadn't flown the plane in exhibitions for two years, and his brief use of it at Crowley had convinced him it needed work. "Seems a little down on power," he told Rich, "though that could be because I'm so used to the Bucher, now. Compression doesn't check out too bad. I'd like to pull the heads and have a look, but there isn't time."

It was Monday evening, and Rich had stayed to help with the plane. "I haven't noticed anything really wrong with it," he told Carlie.

"No, you're used to it this way. The feel is off for me, though. I'm going to have to learn her all over again in the next few days. And we'll work on these wires and control surfaces at night." He hesitated, looking at Rich. "That is, if you're sure you want to put in the extra time."

"Of course. Why not?"

Carlie shrugged. "Just thought you might have other plans."

"Well, actually, Friday night . . . but I can cancel that, I guess."

"The Svanne girl?"

Rich nodded.

"No need to cancel. We should be finished by Friday. At least, we'd better be."

Rich went to the workbench to get some tools, then came back to White Arrow and began removing the engine cowling. After a minute, he stopped work. He looked down at Carlie, who was busy blocking up the wheels. "Could I ask you something?" he said.

"Sure."

"I'd like your opinion about this business with me and Josie. I don't know whether I should try to explain it to Tommy, or not."

"Explain what?"

"About her and me. The way I feel."

"Kind of stuck on her, huh?"

Rich smiled at the phrase. "I guess so, I'm not sure. I know I like being around her. I want her to like me, though I don't know if she really does. If she does . . . well, I suppose I'd just have to tell Tommy how things are."

"Why?"

Rich shrugged. "You know how he feels about the Svannes."

"Not really. I know how he feels about Jake, but that's not the same thing."

"I guess not."

"Anyway, I don't figure it's Tommy you're worrying about."

"What?" Rich frowned—then nodded slowly. "Yeah, you're right. It's Debbie." He hadn't let himself think about this much. He liked Debbie, always had. But having seen so much of her during the past two years, he'd started thinking of her as just a friend, not someone special like Jocelyn. "She hasn't even spoken to me since what happened yesterday. How did I know Josie was going to show up? I think she's been avoiding me too."

"I'm afraid I can't give you much advice. That's not my strong suit."

He looked at Carlie curiously. "You've never been married, I guess, have you?"

Carlie stopped work. He sat holding the wheel he'd just removed from the axle, looking at nothing. "Once," he said softly, and laid the wheel down.

"Oh." He was sorry he'd asked the question. He hadn't meant to pry. He was about to apologize when Carlie went on:

"It didn't take, though. I'd started show-flying by then, and there was too much traveling, too little security—no kind of life for a woman." He massaged his temples with the thumb and fingers of one hand. He'd had a headache after the crash, and it still bothered him. "This isn't much of a life for anyone, I guess, when you come right down to it."

"I like it," Rich said.

Carlie didn't answer immediately. He'd begun disassembling the brake mechanism from the back of White Arrow's wheel; when he spoke again, he continued working.

"I guess the thing with me is, I never liked timetables. Could never follow that little row of numbers from where I was to where I was going. I'd always see some place else along the way that interested me, and forget where I was headed. Hadn't been for that, I might have been with one of the big lines—got myself a nice set of captain's stripes, thirty thousand dollars a year, and a girl in every port." He laughed to himself.

"Who wants an airline captain who can't follow a time-table? If I had to do it over, maybe I'd learn—or maybe not. This life is all right. I like it, I guess—except for the crowds."

This wasn't the first time Rich had heard Carlie refer to "crowds" in that tone of voice. It had puzzled him. This seemed as good a time as any to ask: "What's wrong with them?"

"Crowds? Nothing much." He gave the wheel halves a vicious rap to separate them. "As long as you don't mind being watched by a bunch of vultures."

"I don't get that."

Carlie looked up again. "Why do you think they come to see us? To watch us fly? You think they pay good money for an exhibition of the fine art of aerobatics? Like hell! They come to see one of us smack the ground. When we don't, they're disappointed. You heard the hand I got after I smashed the Bucher, didn't you?"

Rich was shocked. "But that was when they saw you weren't hurt. . . . No, I think you're wrong, Carlie, I don't think that's why they come."

"I do. It's why they like the clown act best—because he looks like he's going to crash all the time."

"Yes, but—"

Carlie threw down a wrench, and pivoted to face him. "But you've got your mind made up, haven't you? You really want to be in this business, don't you?" When Rich hesitated, Carlie laughed harshly and said, "If you had good sense, you'd take those ratings you've earned and find some place that would pay you decent money for them." He turned away again. "Of course, it's up to you. If you want to stick around, I'll teach you what I know. Maybe you'll make it as a clown flier too."

Carlie gathered up his tools and the wheel parts, and stood. "But understand something. That's all you'll ever be, because that's all any of us in this business are. We paint our planes instead of our faces, and turn cartwheels in the sky instead of a sawdust ring. Sky clowns, performing in a flying circus, while the crowd waits to see if one of those falls will really hurt. The sooner you find out that's how it is, the better off you'll be. . . ."

The subject wasn't mentioned again the rest of that week. They talked very little. Rich continued to think about what had been said as they worked in the evenings, but he didn't want to discuss it. He was almost afraid of what else Carlie might say. But Carlie was quiet too, unusually so, almost as if he'd shocked himself a little. And he was still troubled by headaches.

Fortunately, no complicated work was required on White Arrow, and by Thursday night only a few minor details remained to be taken care of. They finished Friday afternoon. Later that same evening, Rich checked out the 172, and flew it to Wichita.

He landed at Municipal Airport and left the plane in the transient parking area. The evening was warm, and he found Jocelyn waiting in her convertible with the top down. "Hi," he said, "hope I'm not late."

"Hi." She glanced at her watch as he got into the car. "No—are you ever?"

He laughed. "Well, I used to be, for almost everything. Flying changes you, though. You get to where you watch the clock pretty close."

"That's nice," she said, starting the engine and pulling briskly out into traffic.

He looked at her more closely. She was wearing a shapeless, ankle-length gown in patchwork colors; a long-sleeved jacket of black felt; and the blocky, barge-shaped shoes that were popular that year. The whole outfit was fashionable, he guessed, and probably expensive, but he couldn't help wondering why modern styles made a woman look as though she'd dressed at a Goodwill store, in the dark. She looked pretty in spite of her clothes—though he had the feeling she was a little annoyed about something. He didn't know what.

She drove rapidly, as was her habit, and not especially well. She weaved through traffic, cut signals too close, and was unsparing of the car's shrilly plaintive horn. At a busy intersection, she swept past several cars just as the light was changing, and began a left turn; there were still a few pedestrians in the crosswalk and she honked at them furiously. When the male member of a middle-aged couple turned to glare at her, she knifed by, missing them by inches, shouting a curse over her shoulder.

Rich said, "For Pete's sake, what's the hurry?"

"Richie," she said, without taking her eyes from the road, "try not to be tiresome tonight, will you?"

He said nothing else. She was in the worst mood he'd seen, up to now, and he decided it would be best not to argue. Like as not, she'd come out of it once they got to the party.

Jocelyn pulled to a curb-scuffing stop in front of an ultramodern apartment building. The place was fronted by palm trees and rock-lined planters, and illuminated by lawn-level lights. They entered a court-yard through a Spanish-style arch, passed a fish pond surrounded by ferns and moss, and paused beside a wall-mounted intercom. Jocelyn pressed a button under the name Barrett; the lock securing a massive wrought-iron door clicked. They went through a lobby and down a hallway, finding the door to the apartment open when they got there. An incredible volume of noise was issuing from inside: shouts and laughter competing with the raucous squall of a rock combo. "Hi, sweetheart!" Deke Barrett said.

He stood with a drink in one hand and the other arm around Tina; he was dressed in cut-velvet pants, red against purple, and had on a florid print shirt that looked capable of glowing in broad daylight. He draped the hand with the drink in it around Jocelyn's shoulders, kissed her with too much enthusiasm, and said, "Come on in, we're just getting started."

The party seemed further advanced than that; the room was jammed with people who were dancing, or standing and talking—shouting, actually—with drinks in their hands, and there was no way to move through the room without bumping into someone. Nobody seemed to mind.

The apartment itself amazed Rich; the main room was oval-shaped, with a free-standing staircase between it and what looked like a kitchen. Stairs led up to a balcony suspended from the wall, with rooms opening off of it. There was no real furniture in evidence, only long, upholstered pads and a scattering of cushions along the walls—but the most remarkable feature was a raised, stonework basin in the center of the room with a palm tree growing out of it. The tree was almost tall enough to touch the two-storey ceiling. Rich wasn't sure he'd want to live here—but neither had he realized that television announcers made as much money as Barrett obviously did.

He became separated from Jocelyn when Deke pulled her away to meet someone, then lost the two of them in the crowd. He edged closer to one wall, where he could look at the other guests, recognizing a few from the Svannes' pool party. Most were strangers. Everyone had on mod clothing of some sort, and he was sorry he'd come in sportscoat and slacks. He was still thinking about this when he felt someone take him by the arm, and looked around to find Susu next to him.

"Hi, Richie!" she cried above the din. "Nice to see you!"

"Nice to see you, Susu!" he bellowed back.

She started to say something else, then gave up and tugged his arm, gesturing with her head for him to follow. They shouldered their way toward the back of the room. They went through a door to another room, almost as crowded as the first but shielded somewhat from the stereophonic roar of the record player. There was a set of French doors on the far side, opening onto a terrace, while the back wall was taken up by a full-length bar. Susu led him to the bar where two men in red jackets were mixing drinks, and ordered something for herself. "What'll you have?" she asked.

He rarely drank, not caring that much for the taste. Besides, he flew so regularly there weren't many times when it was safe. He was feeling depressed by Jocelyn's desertion though, and grateful for Susu's company, so he ordered a light bourbon with ginger ale. He followed the girl out to the terrace, and they stood by the railing, looking down at the garden and swimming pool.

"Wow," she said. "Mob scenes bug me, you know?"

"It's quite a gathering," he agreed.

"I mean, like, what can you do? You can't really talk to anybody, with all that noise. You can't even dance without getting lost. You might as well be by yourself, you know?"

"The lonely crowd," he said.

"What? Oh; right. All Deke's parties are like this."

She was a little younger than he'd thought at first. She was wearing a black-velvet vest over a white blouse, and black short-shorts (of the two extremes in fashion, he much preferred this one). She had a good figure—somewhat short-waisted, with very long legs —and her face was pretty too. As much as he could see of it. She wore her dark glasses day and night, apparently.

"Why do you come?" he asked.

"Oh, everybody does. You get to meet everyone who's important. Like, you're here, right?"

He wasn't sure how to take this, but he nodded.

"Only, it doesn't do much good," she went on. "I mean, you meet interesting people, and try to get to know them, and they act like they're friends, but they're not, right? It's just eat, drink, and be merry, for tomorrow is another day. . . . And they say they'll phone you, but they don't. You know?"

"I guess so," he said.

"I'm a model," she added, as though this explained things.

Rich felt sorry for her, without being sure why. He couldn't think of anything to talk about, but was unwilling to walk away and leave her; she seemed content with silence, so he stood and sipped his drink slowly to make it last. What else was there for him to do, go looking for Jocelyn? In a way, he would have liked to—but he couldn't.

Deke Barrett appeared at the entrance to the terrace, saw them, and motioned. "Come on up to the study," he said. "We've got something special."

Rich wasn't sure the invitation included him, but he let Susu pull him with her. They went back through the front room, up the stairs and along the balcony to a door. There were several people in the room when they entered, and one of them was Jocelyn.

Inside, Deke Barrett closed the door and locked it.

Chapter 10

It was a small room, originally a den or guest bedroom perhaps, that had been changed into something quite different. There was a large window frame on the back wall, with a photographic enlargement of New York City behind it, and a great many color posters and black-and-white blowups of silent film stars on the adjoining walls. The furnishings consisted of a huge circular couch, a conventional sofa, and several floor cushions; there was a color television set, a small cabinet bar, and a tape-deck console with shelves of recordings. The air was heavy with the smell of burning incense, a thick, resiny fragrance that made the quarters seem even closer and more intimate. Deke Barrett had referred to the room as "the study"—but with no desk, no bookcases, not even a reading lamp in sight, Rich wondered just what it was he studied.

They found places on the sofa, and after he and Susu were settled, Rich looked around to see who else was present. He recognized the three sitting on the floor beneath the New York skyline: the dark-haired

Tina, the actorish Don, and Dodie Boyle, the girl he'd
met at the Svannes'. A man he didn't know was at
the far end of the sofa, while Jocelyn reclined on the
circular couch, propping herself on one arm. She was
looking at Rich, smiling faintly.

"Having a nice time?" she asked, eyeing Susu.

He nodded. He still didn't know what was wrong
with her tonight.

"Beautiful!" Deke Barrett said. He turned up the
volume of the tape machine. The music was East
Indian, thin and reedy, and Rich didn't care for it
much. Barrett touched a wall switch and the normal
lights went out, replaced by the eerie glow of an
ultraviolet lamp. It touched cold fire from the wall
posters and painted the Manhattan sky an ominous,
radioactive purple. Deke Barrett knelt near the end
of the sofa, and the man sitting there handed him a
lighted cigarette. Deke said, "Too *much!*"

But Rich wasn't paying a lot of attention to what
Deke said or did; he was wondering if it was up to
him to go across and sit beside Jocelyn. Did she expect
him to? The question troubled him because, although
they'd come together and he'd thought of her as his
date for the evening, she'd behaved as though this
weren't so. She'd behaved as though they were strangers, or as though she were angry with him. Why?
Over what?

He could think of nothing he'd said or done that
would account for it—yet he felt almost as miserable
and self-conscious as if he'd been guilty. Guilty of

something over which he had no control, only of being himself, perhaps.

"Richie . . . ? Susu was touching his arm, offering him something. "Here." A cigarette; a slender, misshapen cylinder of pale brown paper. He knew immediately what it was and shook his head. Susu leaned forward to pass the cigarette to Deke Barrett.

Barrett was sitting cross-legged on the floor. He smiled at Rich and said, "Go ahead, man, it's good stuff. The best, I mean. Grade-A gold, uncut."

"Thanks," Rich said, "but I don't smoke."

Some of the others laughed. Don said, "That's different. Smoking will kill you, man; this won't."

"It's easy," Susu told him. "I'll show you how."

"I'd rather not."

It was as simple as that, really. He preferred not to. The experience might be pleasant—he was sure it was, in fact, in the same sense that alcohol could simulate brief, pleasant feelings. But both substances acted on the mind, and that was what he didn't like; as long as brains came one to a customer, he didn't intend to play around with his.

"Thanks anyway."

"Oh, for heaven's sake!" Jocelyn said. She swung her feet to the floor and sat up, glaring at him. "The least you can do is try it. Everyone else is."

"Yes, I know." He knew this argument and didn't believe it. "That's fine by me, really—I don't object."

"Nice of you," Deke Barrett said, and grinned at the others.

"Look—" He welcomed a feeling of annoyance; it was relief from the pressure being exerted against him. "All I mean is, it's your business, your decision, and I respect it."

"But you think it's wrong," someone said.

"No. I know it's illegal, of course, but I'm not smart enough to tell people what's right and wrong for them. So long as they don't hurt anyone else, it's their affair. I have all I can handle, trying to make my own decisions, and this—" he gestured to the cigarette Deke was holding, "—is one of them."

His statement seemed to end the argument. Jocelyn shrugged and lay back on the couch; Deke went to change the tape, which had stopped playing, and the others began a quiet conversation.

Barrett came back, sat on the couch beside Jocelyn, and began massaging her neck with one hand. She was still looking at Rich. She took the stub of the cigarette from Deke, drew on it, and exhaled slowly. After a moment, she said, "You really . . . actually . . . are. Aren't you?"

"What?" Rich asked.

"As square as you seem to be."

"Go easy, Josie," Deke Barrett said.

"Oh, it's nothing to be ashamed of. In some ways, it's rather charming. I said that, didn't I? Didn't I tell you he was rather charming?" When no one answered, she looked at Rich from hooded eyes. "I rather liked that about you. It was—different. The trouble is, it doesn't wear too awfully well. It's my fault, I should have known. I'm sorry, Richie dear."

Curiously, he felt no anger for her. Later, he knew, he'd feel it for himself. There was so much that he, too, should have known, and hadn't; so many ways he'd let himself be blinded. He'd seen only what he wanted, only her physical beauty and the luxury surrounding her—he'd made himself ignore the rest. What was happening now didn't really surprise him. "I'm sorry too," he said, and stood up. "Is there a phone I can use to call a cab?"

Deke Barrett didn't look at him. "In the bedroom, end of the hall."

He'd forgotten the door was locked and pulled at it a couple of times before remembering. He turned the latch and went out. As he was going down the hall, he heard someone close it, but didn't look back. He was surprised when Susu caught up with him.

Sounding a little out of breath, she said, "Hey, you don't have to do that. I've got my car here. I'll drive you."

"Thanks, don't bother. A cab is fine."

"Why spend the money? I mean, I'd like to get out for a while anyway, you know? Really."

He stopped, and looked at her.

"Come on. . . ," she said.

Her car was small, noisy, and dilapidated. One of those older-model British sedans that carry on in life like punched-out fighters: weaving slightly, mumbling strangely, but forging ahead. Susu coaxed it into one more bout with the road.

They drove for a while, then the girl said, "Sorry about Josie, and all. That's just the way she is. Everybody knows about her and, like, puts up with it. I guess you didn't though, huh?"

"I'd just as soon not talk about it, all right?"

"Oh, sure."

She turned a corner and shifted through the gears again.

"Sure, I understand," she said. "Wow, I ought to, that sort of stuff is always happening to me. I mean, like, I think some guy digs me a lot, see, and—" She glanced at Rich and saw him frowning. "Oh. Sorry," she said.

He shrugged. "That's okay."

Her next silence lasted all of a minute.

"Actually, they're a bunch of conformists—all that talk about doing your own thing. But if someone comes along who doesn't want to do *their* thing, then—wow, look out! Right? . . . Oh, heck. I'm sorry!"

He grinned. "Go on," he told her.

"Yeah, well, you know. You can dress how you want, say what you want, do anything that turns you on—as long as you dress and talk and do what they do. It really gets me. You hear people say that if Christ came back, the 'straights' would crucify him because of his long hair and bare feet. I think the 'hips' might get him first, because he wouldn't wear bell bottoms or turn on with them."

He laughed aloud.

"I hope you don't think I'm sacrilegious, or anything."

"No, I don't," he said. "I enjoy listening to you."

"Me? Oh-h-h. . . ," she said teasingly.

By the time they reached the airport, Rich found he was feeling better; what had happened at Deke's didn't seem to matter quite so much. He turned to Susu after she stopped the car, and said, "Thanks—for the ride, and everything."

"Oh, sure."

On impulse, he said, "May I see something?" and gently removed her dark glasses. She blinked and smiled.

"Myopia," she said.

"You have pretty eyes."

She shifted uncomfortably. "Well, light bothers them. You know?"

"Susu, I have to do some thinking—try to figure a few things out for myself. There's the show to do this weekend, and I'll be going right back to El Dorado after, and. . . . What I mean is, I probably won't be calling you."

"I know. I understand."

He kissed her, and she returned it generously. Then he got out of the car and went inside.

After breakfast Saturday morning he walked over to the field. It was early, but the flying fraternity had begun to gather. A large turnout was expected for the three-day weekend, and everywhere he looked was evidence of busied preparations. Small planes were circling in the pattern like vultures over carrion, waiting to land; private pilots were coming from all over the country. Already, the transient parking area was three-quarters filled, and late arrivals would end up being diverted to other fields. The parking lots were filling rapidly too, some of the space having been lost to a children's carnival—miniature roller coaster, Ferris wheel, carousel, and a merry-go-round of tiny planes for tiny pilots.

Rich entered the main grounds through an auto gate. He walked back between two of the larger hangars and emerged in the south transition area, which was a broad section of pavement between the hangars and the general aviation runway. Here, most of the exhibitions had been set up.

The Air Force was on hand with a display of fighters, transports, and support craft: huge, silver ships like giant flying fish, their bodies studded with instruments of death. The Experimental Aircraft Association was represented by two or three dozen home-built ships, everything from sleek, low-wing jobs to World War I replicas, to tiny Volkswagen-powered single-seaters. And the antique aircraft buffs were on hand too, with an ancient Curtis Robin, a French Saulnier, several Ox-5 Jennies, and many others—some, so perfectly restored, they looked like toys instead of what they were: man's first bold challenges to the sky. Rich strolled slowly, almost reluctantly past the beautiful old planes. Though he'd seen most of them before at other shows, he never tired of looking. If he'd had a dream come true, it would have been to fly each of these wondrous machines.

Hangar Four was at the far end of the general runway. A portion of the floor space in this structure had been reserved for the members of the air show. Maurice Brun's sailplane was there, as well as Jiggs's clipped-wing Cub, and a couple of World War II fighters that would be flown by a Dr. Joe Caughlin. Rich saw the Citabria Decathlon that Tommy had rented for him, and the battered old Ryan trainer he knew belonged to Wilkey Jefferson. Wilkey's act consisted of "flying the wings off"—steering the Ryan through the doors of a makeshift shed, literally destroying the ship—a spectacular and extremely dangerous stunt that Rich, personally, hated. The only ship he didn't see, when he looked for it, was the Tomkins-Waco— White Arrow.

He did see Tommy and some other members of the show though, standing near the door to the hangar office. He went over to join them. " 'Morning," he said to the group in general, and then, to Tommy: "Isn't Carlie here, yet?"

"Hello, Rich. No, he had a couple of things to take care of before coming over. Should be along any time, though."

"Allo, Reech," Maurice Brun said. Jiggs Wilkerson clicked his heels and said, *"Guten Tag, mein Herr."* Debbie smiled and nodded, but didn't speak.

"Is there anything you'd like me to do this morning?" he asked Tommy.

"No, nothing special. Oh—" he took a set of keys from his pocket and handed them over "—you'll want to check out your kite. It's the same as the one you flew at Marysville."

"Okay, thanks."

"You can ask Carlie, when he gets in, if there's anything he wants."

"But you say," Maurice said, picking up the conversation Rich had interrupted, "that nobodee is injure? Carlee is all right, *au moins*?"

"Oh, sure." Tommy glanced at Rich. "I was just telling them about Crowley. . . . No, no one was hurt; Carlie just got a bump on the head, is all."

Jiggs chuckled. "Can't hurt old Carlie there."

"Little different story with the bird," Tommy went on. "I talked to Cap yesterday, and we've got some grief. The constant-speed casing was split open, and that probably means crankshaft damage too."

Jiggs gave a low whistle. "Got to run you two, three thousand."

"Probably more, by the time we're finished with the wings and landing gear and so on."

Rich was stunned by this estimate: he'd had no idea the damage to the Bucher would cost so much.

"Well, I'll just have to worry about that when there's time," Tommy said, "Right now I've got a meeting with the organizers, over at the motel. If anyone wants me, that's where I'll be."

He and Debbie left together.

Maurice excused himself to go back to work waxing his sailplane, which left only Jiggs and Rich. "What do you say to a cup of coffee, shtudent?" Jiggs asked.

"Thanks, but I'd better wait around for Carlie."

"No problem. We sit by the window, we can see him when he comes in."

"Well . . . all right, then."

The coffee shop was busy. They had to wait a few minutes to get a seat next to a front window. They waited even longer for the girl who was serving them to clear the table and take their order. "Two coffees," Jiggs told her—then raised a schoolmasterly finger at her and said, "*when* you have time, and not a moment before."

"Thanks," the girl said. "Madhouse today, isn't it?"

"It's that crazy air-show bunch," Jiggs informed her seriously.

After their coffees came, Jiggs said, "What's with you, this morning? You look as though you're practicing to be a cigar store Indian—Chief Woodenface himself."

Rich forced a smile. "Sorry. Guess I've had a few things on my mind."

"Okay, give. What's the trouble?"

He hesitated a moment. Part of what was bothering him—the personal part—was something he couldn't discuss, no matter how much he wanted to. But there was something else that had been on his mind, nagging at him, and Jiggs seemed just the person to ask. "Would you tell me something? Your honest opinion, I mean—about people who pay to see the show we put on."

"Yeah?"

"Did it ever occur to you that they might come, hoping to see someone get hurt? Maybe not consciously, just secretly, but. . . ."

"The Hatcher Theory of bloodthirsty audiences, you mean." When Rich looked startled, Jiggs grinned. "I've heard him on the subject."

"But you don't believe it?"

"Hell, I don't even think Carlie believes it. Not entirely, anyhow. The only time he talks that way is when he's feeling low for some reason."

Rich nodded. "This was after Crowley."

"That might explain it. You have to understand, Carlie's lost some friends to this business. We all have, of course, but it seems to hit him harder. There's some bitterness, and since he can't take it out on any one person, he takes it out on the crowd. That's everybody, so it's no one, see?"

"I think so."

Jiggs looked thoughtful. "As to what people might think about us secretly, as you put it, I just don't know. One guess is probably as good as another. I'll tell you what mine is. I think people like to see us take a chance, and somehow it's important that we could get hurt doing it, but I think they want to see us get away with it. It would be less fun if someone really got hurt.

"Take my routine, for instance. People think, Gee, that might happen to me if I tried to fly without knowing how. When I do get down in one piece, they're relieved, and happy. I think it's that way with the whole show—people don't want to see the lion bite, they just want to know it has teeth."

Rich was feeling much better by the time Jiggs had

finished. He sensed that the other man had put into words something he himself had felt, and believed, but didn't know how to say.

He felt good most of the rest of the day—until near the end of it.

That day's show went well. The crowd was as large as hoped for, and in holiday spirits: eager and willing to be pleased. Even the weather seemed to conspire favorably, it was warm enough by early afternoon to provide Maurice with good thermals—upward air currents—for his glider routine. He dazzled the spectators with graceful figures flown in almost eerie silence, only the faint hiss of wind over the sailplane's glassy surfaces. When he was finished, a light breeze picked up and blew parallel to the runway, favoring the other performers.

The day's events concluded with an appearance by the Blue Angels, guiding their Air Force jets back and forth above the field in a flashing, intricate, thunderous display of close-formation aerobatics. Rich paused to watch the performance, having returned to Hangar Four early to take care of his plane. He admired the Angels even though he had no great desire to fly jets himself. He wasn't that impatient to get where he was going, when he flew. The jet team concluded its act, and after that, Rich wheeled his gaudy little aerobat back into the hangar.

He found a parking space for it between a couple of other planes. He'd locked the cabin door and started toward the front of the hangar when he saw the Tomkins group coming in, wheeling White Arrow.

Skip and Carlie were in front, towing the Tomkins-Waco by its wing struts. Maurice and Jiggs walked next to the plane. Tommy and Debbie followed at a short distance, walking in silence. In fact, going out to meet them, it occurred to Rich that everyone seemed very quiet. "Let me give you a hand," he said. "There's a space for her over by this wall. . . ."

He saw that Skip and Carlie had come to a halt, the plane still on the hangar apron. They stood staring at it, and after a moment Rich saw what the others did. There was a dark spot on the lower lip of the engine cowling, a shiny, uneven streak that ran back along the underside of the nacelle, gathered at the rim, and dripped down on the gray concrete. Oil.

Rich looked at Tommy.

"Number five cylinder," the older man said. "Let go just as Carlie finished the ribbon pick-up."

Rich went closer to the plane, reached out and touched the stained fuselage, then rubbed his fingers together as though this made the disaster real. For it was a disaster. Without a biplane for such stunts as the wing walk and ribbon pick-up, they had no show; without a show tomorrow, they would lose their contract; and without the money from this performance, the Tomkins International Air Show was finished.

Chapter 11

"We ought to be able to find a piston and barrel around here, somewhere. Or I could shoot over to El Dorado, and. . . ." Rich's voice trailed off as he saw the slow shake of Tommy's head.

Carlie said, "Wake up, Rich. The rod put a hole in the block. Where do you think all that oil is coming from?"

He shook his head. Yes, of course—he should have realized. The whole engine was shot, he wasn't thinking clearly.

Debbie said, "Dad, sit down," and drew him toward one of the chairs near the office entrance. Tommy sank into it, put his elbows on his knees, and rested his head against his knuckles. No one said anything, and after a moment he looked up.

"Got to find us another bird. *Got* to! Trouble is, the only ones I can think of are too far away. Anyone got any ideas?"

"I saw a Steerman this morning," Skip said, "down at the east end of the field."

"Forget that," Jiggs said. "It's an old crop duster, not even in license anymore."

"Pete Taliaferro?" Carlie asked.

"Out on the West Coast," Tommy told him. "He couldn't possibly get here in time."

"Well, we've got the Decathlon, don't forget," Rich said.

Tommy shook his head. "For one thing, there's no way to rig it for the wing walk. For another, people who come to an air show expect to see a bipe. They're not going to sit and watch you fly a plane that most can't tell apart from a Piper Cub."

"We may have to try it," Carlie said, "if nothing else turns up."

"We may; but I hope not. I think I might be in some trouble with the organizers. There's a nonperformance clause in our contract." He looked around at them bleakly. "Well, I'll get on the phone and see what I can find. Any of the rest of you have any ideas, ring me in my room."

The group began to break up.

Tommy, Debbie, and Carlie started back to the motel; Jiggs and Maurice decided to go into town for dinner. Rich stayed to help Skip bring his gear inside, and afterward walked back with him. "Are you going anywhere with the car tonight?" he asked.

Skip shook his head. "Thought I'd have dinner in my room, watch some TV, and turn in early. Why, you want it?"

"If you wouldn't mind."

"Sure." Skip handed him the keys. "Got something on in town, huh?"

"In a way," Rich agreed.

He turned up the long, curving driveway and stopped in front of the house. In the fading light it looked even larger and more forbidding than he remembered. He wished desperately he could think of someone else to ask for help, but he couldn't, so he got out of the car and went up to the door.

A maid answered his ring. She listened to his request, went away for a minute, then returned to inform him that Mr. Svanne would see him.

She ushered him along the hall and through a door to the business magnate's office. The room was large and luxuriously furnished, lighted by a glow from the fireplace and from the lamp above the vast desk that dominated one end of the room. "Urgent business, huh?" Jake Svanne said, not looking up from the stack of papers on his desk. "Sit down, be with you in a minute."

Rich chose a chair near the desk, angled so he could see about the room. The heads of several wild animals were mounted on the walls. They stared at him with glassy-eyed ferocity—as though wishing for a second chance.

"Okay. . . ." Jake Svanne pushed the pile of papers aside and looked at his watch. "It's a little late, but never too late for business. What's on your mind?"

He'd hoped to find the man a little friendlier, the

way he'd seemed the last time they met. He guessed the word "business" had made a difference. "I'd like to rent your plane from you," he said. "I need it the rest of this weekend."

"My plane?"

"The Great Lakes, I mean." For a moment he'd forgotten that the man owned dozens of planes. "I'd be willing to pay anything within reason for it."

"You would?" Svanne tilted his chair back and folded his arms. He looked thoughtful. "Man comes in at an odd hour of the evening, and wants to rent a plane. Not just any plane, a biplane. Man's with an air show playing in town, and is willing to pay anything within reason." He nodded to himself. "I see. . . . Anybody get hurt?"

"No. Just blew the engine."

"Glad that's all. It's bad enough, I guess. You lost that German-built ship last week, up near Denver. Now the old Waco—what did he call it?—White Arrow. Bad news all around, I'd say."

"You make it sound like carelessness, or negligence," Rich objected. "It wasn't. Carlie's the best pilot in the country."

"Well, one of the best. I wasn't questioning that."

"Look, I'd take good care of the plane, I guarantee you. We probably wouldn't fly it more than a couple of hours, total, and I'd clean it afterwards personally, and. . . ."

Jake Svanne was shaking his head. "No deal," he said.

"I see." He realized, suddenly, that he hadn't expected any other answer—and wondered why he felt so disappointed. "There's nothing that might make you change your mind?"

"Not unless you can give me a lot better reasons than I think you can. I don't rent aircraft, and if I did, I wouldn't rent my personal plane. *If* I rented it, it wouldn't be to somebody who was going to fly upside down a few feet off the ground. As far as you guaranteeing me anything—I don't mean to offend you—but I doubt you can. Even if you could afford the insurance, it would be next to impossible to replace the Lakes if anything should happen to it. I'm sorry for your sake, but that's how it is."

"Sure." He stood up. "Thanks anyway."

"You in a hurry to go somewhere?"

"No."

"Sit down for a minute then," Jake Svanne said. He leaned forward, crossing his arms on the desk, his brow creased in thought. "Things are going to be pretty tough for Tommy now. All it needed was a run of bad luck to finish him off, and now it looks like he's got it. Sort of leaves you on the spot, doesn't it?"

"How do you mean?"

The older man shrugged. "Just that Tommy can't afford you anymore. There must be fifty guys with their own airplanes who could fly your part of the show. Guys who'd do it for next to nothing, just for the fun. Instead, Tommy's been renting a plane for you, paying your expenses, and giving you credit for all the air time you spend practicing. Pretty nice deal—for you."

"I work around the field," Rich said defensively, "and give some lessons too."

"For which you're paid, right?"

"Well. . . ."

Svanne smiled. "Tommy's a nice man. He's a nice man, and he likes you, and that's too bad for both of you. Because it hurts him financially, and it sure isn't doing you much good. Not unless you're planning to spend the rest of your life pumping fuel and giving flying lessons. You aren't, are you?"

"No. Of course not." But in truth he'd been troubled, lately, by questions surprisingly like the ones Jake Svanne was asking. He'd tried to tell himself, on paydays, that he was earning his keep, and tried to persuade himself that all the flight time he logged was for the good of the show. But was it, really? Or was it in fact costing Tommy too much, and had he become a burden to the man he owed so much? Jake Svanne seemed to know the answer to these questions—and suddenly he knew them too.

Svanne said, "I told you once before and I'll tell you again. I'm always in the market for a good man, and I like what I've seen of you, so far. I like the way you handle yourself in difficult situations. That's why I say, if you should decide it's time to give yourself —and Tommy—a break, I'd like to know about it."

"You're offering me a job?"

"More or less."

"I see. What kind?"

The older man spread his hands, palms up. "That isn't important at the moment. Not to me, at least. Once a man joins the organization, I don't have much trouble finding out what he's best at. Are you interested?"

He said nothing for a minute; the question was too sudden. He'd need time to make up his mind. He'd have to think a little more about Tommy's difficulties, and about his own future, and what was best for both of them. . . . "When would I be expected to start?" he asked.

Svanne's eyes narrowed. He gazed at Rich intently for a moment. Then, as though satisfied with what he saw, he nodded once, and said, "Give Tommy all the notice he wants. He'll be reasonable. He may be sorry as the devil to see you go—I guess he will—but he'll know it makes sense. He won't try to keep you around any longer than necessary."

"That may not be any time at all, then. The way things stand, he may not even have a show, after tomorrow. Unless you'll change your mind about renting the Great Lakes."

Jake Svanne shook his head.

"You could call it a bonus for signing a new man," Rich went on. "You say it's your personal ship, but I'll bet it's registered to the company—and I'm part of the company now, aren't I?"

"Now, wait a minute—"

"As far as renting it to someone to fly stunts in, it *is* a stunt plane, isn't it? You wouldn't want it used for crop dusting, would you? Besides, if you rent it out, you can declare it as an expense on your income taxes, and—"

"*Hold on!*" Jake Svanne leaned his head against one hand, eyes closed. "I had every intention of putting you to work in one of the operational branches—freight, charter passenger, or something of the sort."

There was a pause, and Rich said, "Yes?"

"You're leaving me no choice but to put you into the sales department." Jake Svanne opened the top drawer of his desk and took something out. He slid an object across the desk top: a small, silver key. "Just see to it you get her back to me in one piece, understand?"

"*Yes*, sir."

"Otherwise, I'll put you to work washing D-C 10's with a toothbrush."

"Yes, *sir!*"

Jake got up and walked Rich to the door of the studio. Opening it, he paused and said, "Incidentally, what's this I hear about you and Josie? You're not getting on?"

The events of the day had wiped all thoughts of Jocelyn from his mind. Now he remembered—and his heart sank as it occurred to him Jake might not know how complete the break was. If he knew, would it change things? "I—I'm afraid that's right," he admitted.

"Good. Oh, I know, she's my daughter, and I love her. But she's going to be a problem for some fella, and I intend keeping you too busy for that." He clapped Rich on the shoulder, and with the same gesture steered him out to the hall. "Call me when you're ready to start," he said, and shut the door.

He drove back to the airport motel slowly. There was so much to think about. He could hardly believe what he'd just done; it was impossible to guess all the changes it would mean. Two years, now, he'd been with the Tomkins International Air Show, two of the best and most exciting years of his life. Now it was over, and that didn't seem possible. For a moment it seemed to him he'd made a terrible mistake, but thinking again of the reasons that had led to his decision, he knew he'd done the right thing. What was hard to understand was why it hurt so much.

He had one more difficult thing to do that night. When he reached his room, he picked up the phone and asked for Tommy. "Hi, it's me. Any luck yet?"

"No. No, but I haven't given up. I'm still looking. And if it comes down to it—well, we'll go with the Decathlon, and I'll talk it up good on the PA. Don't you worry."

He wanted very badly to tell Tommy about the Great Lakes, but he couldn't. For one thing, if he told him that, he'd have to tell him about quitting, too, and he didn't think he was able tonight. Besides, he didn't want Tommy to start worrying about accepting help, however indirectly, from Jake Svanne. He wanted to put that off as long as possible.

"I won't worry," he said. "All that matters is that we give folks a good show. Right?"

"That's the spirit! You get some sleep, now."

"Good night, Tommy."

He woke up feeling feverish and a little frightened. He wasn't sure why. Then he remembered what he had to do today, and he knew why. He groaned, rubbed his eyes, and got out of bed.

The worst part was, there was too much time. He wished he could go back to sleep for a couple of hours, but knew he couldn't. He ordered breakfast sent to his room, then sat over it for a long while, not eating much. The phone rang once but he didn't answer.

Later, he called the front desk and left a message. "For Mr. Tomkins in Room 1217. 'Have biplane for today's show . . . perfect condition, ready to fly . . . will be at field with it just after noon . . . signed, Rich.' This is very important," he told the desk clerk. "If Mr. Tomkins isn't in his room, page him, please."

The clerk assured him the message would be delivered.

He watched television until it was time to go, then slipped down the back stairs to the parking lot, making sure he wasn't seen. He got into Skip's car and drove away. He headed south through the city, stopping once to get gas for the car.

The trip to Tri-Cities Field took nearly an hour through moderately heavy Sunday morning traffic. When he arrived, he parked behind the familiar small hangar, putting the car where it would remain in shade most of the day. He locked it, then walked around front. The Lakes was where he expected it to be, sitting on the apron, looking even more beautiful than the last time he'd seen it; and he walked near to touch the lower wing and slide his palm along the glass-slick fabric.

"Mr. Newman?"

He turned and saw the mechanic, one he hadn't seen before, coming toward him. He nodded.

" 'Morning, sir. She's all set to go. Paint ought to be dry by now too."

Rich followed the mechanic's look—then wondered how he'd failed to notice immediately. Just aft of the cockpit was fresh, neat, maroon lettering that read:

TOMKINS INTERNATIONAL AIR SHOW

"He doesn't leave much to chance, does he?" Rich said, and laughed.

"What?"

He shrugged. "Nothing. Say, I'm kind of early, is there someplace I could find a cup of coffee?"

"Machine in the hangar," the mechanic said. "Or, if you're not too fond of warm battery acid, you might prefer to walk up to Operations. They usually have a fresh pot in the lounge."

"Think I'll do that," Rich said, grinning. "Can I get someone to prop for me later?"

"Be here all day."

Rich went up to the operations building. The pilots' lounge on the ground floor was comfortably furnished, and the coffee was good, as advertised. Rich sat near the window, watching the occasional aircraft take off or land, and keeping one eye on the wall clock. It was essential, now, that his timing be exactly right. At 12:30 he got up, waved "thanks" to the operations officer for his coffee, and walked back to where his plane was waiting. Ten minutes later, he was taxiing into position at the head of the runway, radioing for clearance.

"Roger, zero zero Lima," the tower told him, "cleared for take-off. Have a nice day."

"We can't wait for him any longer." Tommy looked at his watch, frowning. He was standing with Debbie, Carlie, and some of the officials of the airport. To Carlie, he said, "Better go on down and make sure the Citabria is ready. Looks like you'll be using it after all."

"I don't understand," Debbie said, frowning. "Rich wouldn't say he'd be here and then—nothing. It isn't like him."

"Something must have come up, sweetheart. I'm sure he'll get here if he can, but—well, we're going to have to start in a few minutes, whether or no."

One of the officials said, "What seems to be the trouble, Mr. Tomkins?"

"No real trouble, Mr. Johnson. Doesn't look like the bipe is going to get here, after all, but nothing to worry about. Just wait'll you see Carlie put that little Decathlon through its paces."

The man named Johnson was chairman of the organizing committee. The news about the loss of White Arrow hadn't pleased him, and now he looked even more skeptical. "See here, Tomkins—" he began.

"Hey, Tommy!" Jiggs was sitting at the announcer's table, using an earplug to listen to VHF radio. The radio was tuned to the control tower frequency. "Someone's coming in. I think it's our boy!"

There was a general movement closer to the table. Someone caught Tommy by the arm and said, "Sir, can you give us a few minutes? Mr. Barrett would like to—"

"Later," Tommy told the man, a member of the television broadcast crew. "Tell him I'll talk to him later." He climbed up onto the platform next to Jiggs. "Hear anything else? Is it him?"

Jiggs pulled the earplug wire out of the radio and turned the volume up. ". . . *Check it down on the field first,*" a voice was saying. *"Continue your approach and report three miles."*

"Zero zero Lima, Roger," another voice said.

"It's him!" Debbie cried.

The direct line to the tower was ringing, and Tommy picked it up. "Hello? . . . Yeah, speaking. . . . Right, we heard. The runway's clear over here, send him in."

As Tommy hung up, the tower controller's voice came over VHF again: *"Zero zero Lima, continue straight in to two four, left. You are clear to land."*

Everyone in hearing distance of the radio let out a cheer. Then they turned to look toward the east end of the field.

The plane was only a speck, at first, hardly visible; but as it slid down the pale blue sky it grew larger, the disk of its engine growing, the knife edges of its wings beginning to glint sunlight.

"It *is*," Tommy murmured with wonder. "It is a bipe."

The plane came in nose high and with power, "dragging" the runway, until it was about a hundred yards from the grandstands. There it cut its power and dropped hawklike to the pavement, rolling to a full stop in front of the stands. With a roar of throttle, it pivoted full circle—then continued to taxi past the applauding crowd.

"Oh, it's beautiful!" Debbie cried. "Just look!" When she turned to her father she saw him staring after the plane, a peculiar look on his face. "What is it?" she asked. "What's wrong?"

He didn't answer. He was climbing down off the announcer's platform, heading for the hangars at a brisk, determined walk.

Carlie stood feet apart, fists planted, and watched the biplane taxi toward him. He'd just reached the hangars when the applause from the crowd had caused him to stop and look back. He'd seen the plane touch down and watched it do its pirouette, recognizing it almost immediately. He was glad to see the airplane but wondered if Rich knew what he was doing.

"I brought you a present," Rich called, after the engine was silent and Carlie had come around beside the cockpit.

"So I see. Cops after you?"

Rich laughed. "Not yet. It's ours for the next two days." He climbed down and stood away so Carlie could mount the wing and look inside the cockpit. "What do you think? Think you can get used to it in time? It flies beautifully."

Carlie stepped back down to the ground. "Shouldn't be any problem. I've flown two or three Lakes before; ought to be able to make friends with this one pretty quick. Provided it's rigged right." He glanced at the plane again. "Considering whose it is, it should be."

"You recognize it, huh?"

"I've seen it a couple of times in the aviation magazines. Then too, I might have been able to figure it out," he said, nodding toward the plane's rudder with its blue TCA emblem. "Tommy didn't have any objections?" Carlie asked.

"Well, actually—" he began, but didn't have a chance to finish.

"*I should have known*," Tommy's voice broke in. They turned to see the owner of the air show striding toward them, followed at a short distance by Debbie, who still looked confused. "Should have been able to figure it out," Tommy growled, stopping and glaring at the plane. "Hell, I know every bipe in this part of the country, and. . . ." He turned on Rich. "The least you could have done was told me."

"Well, I—"

"Never mind. It don't matter. But you could have saved yourself the trouble."

"What?"

"It's a little late in the day for me to start accepting favors from Jake Svanne. I've been getting along all right without him for quite a few years now. Guess I can manage to do it a while longer."

"But this isn't a. . . . I mean, Jake didn't. . . ."

"That's all right, son." Tommy reached out and patted him on the shoulder, not meeting his eyes. "You tried your best. I know you meant well. You just didn't understand the situation."

"I guess I didn't."

Tommy looked at his watch. "Carlie, you'd better get the Decathlon out here. Be set to take off in about . . . oh, let's say about—"

"I guess I still don't," Rich cut in. "Because it isn't like you, Tommy, to be that selfish."

The older man turned slowly. "What, exactly, is that supposed to mean?"

"It means I went to a lot of trouble to get this—" he jerked his thumb at the Great Lakes, "—for you. I rented it, expecting you to pay me back. I have to pay for it whether you use it or not—but that's not what bothers me the most. What bothers me is that, if you don't use it, Carlie will have to do his routine without a biplane; Skip can't do his wing walk at all; the crowd will miss out on half the fun of an air show; and the organizers will probably cancel your contract.

All that, just so you can keep a feud going over something that happened twenty or thirty years ago. Well,
you're right, I don't understand."

For a time, no one said anything. Skip came out
of the hangar carrying his parachutes; he looked at
the others, saw something was wrong, and waited silently to see what it was. Tommy frowned at
Rich—then turned to look at the Great Lakes again.
He moved his shoulders as though shifting them under
some great weight, then he turned to Carlie. "Can
you fly it?"

The pilot shrugged. "Should fly better than White
Arrow, if she's rigged right. Which Rich says she is."

"All right, take-off will be in twenty minutes. Your
regular routine." He faced Rich squarely, looked at
him an instant, then bobbed his head down and up.
"Thanks," he said; and turned and walked away.

Chapter 12

It seemed to him that he flew badly. There was nothing in particular wrong—he stayed in line with his reference points, and began and ended his maneuvers at the correct altitudes—but something was missing. Was it the feel of wind in his face? The hammering of the Warner radial? He found himself stealing glances out the side windows of the Decathlon, admiring or perhaps envying Carlie in the Great Lakes. His own flying felt ragged by comparison.

He was surprised, then, after the opening routine was over, and both planes had landed, when Carlie came over and said, "You looked good today. Real sharp."

"I did? Well, thanks. I wasn't doing anything special."

"Maybe that was it. You seemed smoother than usual, more relaxed. Of course, spending some time in the Lakes could have helped too. Flying a really sensitive ship will sharpen up a good pilot quicker than anything I know."

"I hadn't thought of that."

"Tell you what. We might expand that opening routine of yours; put in some new maneuvers for our next show. I think you're ready to handle a lot more—maybe even start working on a solo now. What would you think of that?"

"Well, I. . . ."

"You don't have to, if you don't think you're ready, of course. I just thought you'd want to."

"Sure, Carlie, I do. And I'm glad you think I could do the job."

How did he tell Carlie that there wasn't going to be a next show for him? How would he go about telling the rest of his friends? Sooner or later, he had to do it, he knew.

He was still looking for the proper words when one of the airport carts came up to them, carrying Skip and Debbie. The girl was driving while Skip sat next to her, half buried in the folds of the parachute he'd used for his jump. He grinned at the others and said, "How's this for riding around in style? My own private chauffeur. Thanks for the lift, doll," he told Debbie as he got out of the cart.

"This is your lucky day," Carlie told him.

"Yeah, how so?"

"There's another car and driver waiting to give you a ride. That nice, shiny convertible over there," he added, pointing to the chase car for the car-to-plane transfer. Skip groaned, and followed Carlie away.

After they'd left, Rich went over to the cart and

gathered up Skip's chute. Debbie picked up the American flag, which was folded on the back seat, and the two of them went into the hangar office. They stowed Skip's things with the rest of the equipment for the show, then turned to leave—and found themselves face to face in an uncomfortable silence.

"Hi," the girl said at last.

He smiled, feeling himself blush. "Hi."

"I was hoping to get a chance to see you for a few minutes. Are you in a hurry?"

"No. Do you want to sit down?"

There was a desk against the far wall. They sat across from each other. After a moment's hesitation, Debbie said, "I just wanted to tell you that Tommy appreciated what you did. He was a little upset at first; but it was a lifesaver. Mr. Johnson told someone there might have been a holdup on payment for the show, otherwise. Tommy will tell you this himself, of course, only. . . . Well, I didn't want you to think he was mad when he wasn't. It took him by surprise, is all."

Rich shook his head slowly. "I know I didn't handle it very well. There must have been a dozen better ways; I just couldn't think of one."

"What amazes me is that you were able to talk Jake Svanne into it."

"I didn't, really. I doubt that anyone talks him into anything he doesn't want to do. I just made a business deal with him."

Debbie seemed thoughtful. "Yes, but for his own,

personal plane? I'm surprised he'd rent it. To anyone except a friend, that is."

"Well, we get along all right. I wouldn't say we were friends, exactly."

"To a friend of Jocelyn's, then."

"What? Oh, I see." When he finally realized what it was she was getting at, he almost laughed. He didn't, though. "The fact of the matter is, Jocelyn and I aren't seeing each other anymore," he told her. "She dropped me, cold."

"Oh, Rich, she didn't!" Debbie said, trying to look disappointed. "How could she?"

"I had the impression it was easy," he said and grinned. He knew, then, that he had to tell her the rest of it. "That isn't important, though. I'm glad it's over. What matters a lot more is—I've decided to leave the show."

"Leave?" she said, not understanding.

"Jake Svanne offered me a job. I've decided to take it."

"But—why?"

"For a couple of reasons. First, I'm not pulling my weight here. When you add it all up, it isn't fair to Tommy."

"He hasn't said so, has he?"

"You know he hasn't, Debs. But you know it's true, anyway."

She looked down. "You said 'a couple' of reasons."

"The other is, I want to start building a career for myself. A real one. Jobs with airlines don't come along every day of the week, you know, and this looks like it could be something pretty good. So . . . I'm going to give it a try."

When she didn't say anything for a moment, he was afraid she was angry. Then she nodded. "I see." She raised her head to look at him. "Does Tommy know?"

"No." He was amazed and troubled to see tears in her eyes. "I just decided last night, and there hasn't been a chance. I—I'd like to tell him myself, though."

"Sure." Debbie drew a breath, and stood up. "I guess it's time I was getting back."

He stood too. "All right. Debbie, I. . . ." He searched for words to tell her that he didn't want this to be the end for them; that he wanted to go on seeing her. As usual, words failed him when he needed them most. "I'll see you later," he said.

After she'd left he sat down again, and remained there a long while, feeling strangely empty.

There was a sound like thunder. It startled him, at first—bad weather was the *last* thing they needed. Then he recognized the sound: Joe Caughlin's P-51 Mustang, taking off for its stunt routine. Tommy had added this act for the Fourth of July show, placing it between the car-to-plane transfer and Skip's wing walk. It meant Skip and Carlie were due in; so Rich went out to meet them.

He took the support bar and the wire-and-leather harness for the wing walk with him. He found the others out beside the Great Lakes, getting it ready. "Climb up and set the brace for me, will you?" Carlie asked when he got there.

"Sure," Rich said. He saw that Carlie was perspiring heavily. His face seemed strained.

"The sun's murder today," Carlie said. "I'm going for a drink of water. You two secure the rig." He walked to the hangar and went inside.

Skip and Rich worked to prepare the plane. Since it had been built for show work, it had the necessary attach points for their equipment. But these were slightly different from the ones on White Arrow, so all the wires and turnbuckles had to be adjusted. As Carlie had said, the sun was fierce, and Rich was feeling a little lightheaded by the time they were done.

When Joe Caughlin finished his flight, and brought the Mustang in, Carlie still hadn't returned. Skip went into the hangar to check, and returned a minute later with his pilot in tow. Skip clambered aboard and began snapping himself into harness; Carlie got into the rear cockpit and signaled Rich for the prop start; and seconds afterward, the Great Lakes was S-turning its way along the taxi strip.

Standing on the top wing, clutching his hold bar like a water skier, Skip Scott waved to the crowd with one hand.

Rich saw them go, then began walking back past the hangars, toward the grandstand area. When the Great Lakes began its take-off—after Tommy's highly dramatic introduction—Rich moved nearer the edge of the runway to watch. It was a performance that always amazed him, because Skip and Carlie made it look so simple. Few of the people watching could imagine just how hard the stunt really was.

As the plane sped down the runway on take-off, Skip waved to the crowd. An instant later, the Lakes was in the air, starting to climb, and no sooner had its wheels left the ground than it began to roll over. This roll had to be performed exactly right, since too fast could tear Skip away from the wing, while too slow could let him fall from it. In either case, even if his harness held, he'd have real trouble getting his footing again.

As usual, Carlie performed the maneuver perfectly.

After a climbing turn, the airplane came back toward the stands. Carlie dived a little to gain speed, then arced upward into an inside loop. He climbed up one side, over the top, and down the back of the loop. And as he pulled out, he rolled inverted once more. He flew the Lakes past the stands upside down, about 50 feet above the ground: so near that when Skip used one hand to wave again, it looked as though he could have touched the grass if he'd wanted. The plane climbed in a wide circle, came back, and started an outside loop.

This was the same as a regular loop, except that the pilot—and his wing walker—went around on the outside. Rich knew from experience how hard it was to fly a good outside loop even without the added burden and extremely high wind resistance of someone standing on the wing. He could only imagine how difficult that extra drag would make it for Carlie.

For that matter, he wondered what it felt like for Skip. To be standing up there on an airplane's wing, just at the top of the loop, looking down at the crowd and the airport and the countryside, as though from the high point on a giant Ferris wheel. . . . To feel oneself propelled forward, and over, and down, down, *down!* toward that flat, unyielding pavement. Screaming down at 120 mph, clinging to a wooden handle attached by wires, feeling the airplane begin to curve under at the bottom of the loop, and your harness tightening on your body, taking your weight. . . . To know, with all that centrifugal force trying to pull you and your plane and its pilot into the ground, that *you* are the lowest part of the combination, the landing gear, in case anything goes wrong!

The crowd roared as Skip waved from the bottom of the loop and the plane began to climb away again. Rich sighed with pleasurable release, knowing the routine was completed. Then he walked back to the exhibition area to find a hamburger stand.

The next performer scheduled was Wilkey Jefferson. Rich watched him from beside the refreshment stand, a little annoyed that he felt the need to watch at all. He disapproved of Wilkey's act. There was, so far as he could see, nothing amusing or trivial, much less entertaining, about a plane crash. Which was all Wilkey really did. He knew Tommy would never have scheduled the act if the organizers hadn't insisted on it; since they had, he figured he might as well see it.

Watching Wilkey take off in the ragged old Ryan, he had to respect the man's guts and confidence, at least. There was nothing easy about what he did—no safe or cautious way to fly an airplane into a solid object—not even at the Ryan's miminum speed of about 50 mph. Several well-known fliers had lost their lives doing it before now. He saw Wilkey bank to turn back, having flown well out to the east of the airport.

The shed that had been erected in the infield looked something like a large outhouse, open at front and back. Inside the loose-board framework were concealed two upright lengths of telephone pole, anchored in the ground. There was also a small explosive charge of black powder. . . . To the east, the Ryan had gone into its long glide, aimed at the shack. . . .

If everything went as planned—if the wind didn't gust or change direction suddenly, if the motor didn't stop or falter, if Wilkey didn't miscalculate more than a few inches during his 100-yard glide—then the plane would plunge through the near opening of the shed, rip its wings off on the phone poles, and then the fuselage and engine and, hopefully, Wilkey, would shoot out the far side. After that, the dynamite would go off for added effect.

This time, all went well during the glide, and to Rich it appeared Wilkey's aim had been good. There was a dull blast, and pieces of shed and some of the Ryan sailed off in various directions. Rich gasped in spite of himself and strained on tiptoes, trying to see through the thick black smoke that swallowed the scene. As it began to drift away, the denuded fuselage of the Ryan became visible, having slid a good twenty yards beyond the destroyed shed. After a long, dramatic pause, Wilkey scrambled from the wreckage, ran to the edge of the runway facing the crowd, and took his bows. The applause was louder than it had been for Skip and Carlie—which further disgusted Rich.

He heard Tommy saying, "In a few minutes now, ladies and gentlemen, we'll introduce to you the great, the amazing, the inimitable Professor Amadeus von Groundloop. . . ."

This surprised Rich. He was sure Jiggs hadn't been scheduled to fly so soon. In fact, he remembered clearly that the next thing on the program was Carlie's aerobatics exhibition. Jiggs was due to fill the space between that and the inverted ribbon pick-up. He was further surprised when a voice that wasn't Tommy's came over the loudspeakers, saying:

"Richard Newman . . . paging Mr. Richard Newman. Please report to the announcer's table. Mr. Richard—"

He arrived out of breath. He saw Tommy and Debbie near the end of the table, with several other people around them. Not until he got closer, though, did he see what was occupying their attention. A man was sitting in a chair, in the shade at the end of the table, head tilted back, eyes closed, a wet cloth across his forehead. It was Carlie Hatcher.

"What's the matter?" he asked when he reached the others. Now he could see a man kneeling beside Carlie, a black bag open near him.

Tommy turned. He ignored Rich's question and said, "I've asked Jiggs to fill in—stretch his routine as long as possible. He ought to be able to give us about fifteen minutes. The Angels are due here at five, and there's no way to get them sooner, which leaves us with close to thirty minutes to fill. Carlie thinks you could do a little something in the Lakes."

He was about to ask again what was wrong with Carlie—but at that moment the pilot opened his eyes and said, "Nothing fancy . . . just buzz around a little." His voice sounded thick and too slow. "Couple low fly-bys, let 'em see the ship . . . 's all. You do that?"

"Sure," Rich said.

"You think you know the bird well enough?" Tommy asked.

"Well enough to do that with it."

Carlie said, "An' after . . . I'll fly the pick-up. Just gotta. . . ."

"I don't think so," the man kneeling in front of him said. He stood up, turning to Tommy. "It's just too much heat, as far as I can tell. That, along with the bump on the head he got last week. I don't think it's anything serious—but I want him inside, out of the sun, the rest of the day at least. He's grounded until I've examined him again."

Carlie started to say something else, but the effort

seemed too much for him. He cursed under his breath and slumped deeper in his chair, glaring at the doctor. Tommy turned back to Rich.

"Okay. Just a few book maneuvers, now—and stay up around 700 or 800. I'll explain to the crowd. Try to give me ten or fifteen minutes of something—anything—all right?"

"Right."

"Here," Tommy said. He fished in his jacket pocket and came up with the key for the Great Lakes.

Chapter 13

Debbie and Skip walked back to the hangar with Rich. They stood and watched as he made a tour of the plane, checking it carefully. "How's fuel?" he asked Skip.

"I checked gas and oil both, right after the wing walk."

"Did Carlie mention any problems?"

Skip shook his head. "Seemed real pleased with her."

Debbie said, "Fifteen minutes is a lot of time to fill. What are you going to do?"

"Darned if I know," Rich admitted. "Whatever comes to mind, I guess. I can start off with the series I fly in the opening, use it to get the feel of things, and then—just improvise. Standard maneuvers. Trouble is, I can't hang them together smoothly, the way Carlies does. Not flying at low altitude, anyway."

"Not too low," Debbie warned.

"I'll watch it."

There was a roar from the grandstands followed by prolonged applause. Skip said, "It sounds like Jiggs has finished up."

"Yeah." Suddenly, Rich was afraid. He knew it was fear because he could remember having felt this way when he first began taking lessons. Those days had been exciting but filled with vague terrors; he could recall watching the treetops as he drove to the field, looking for wind, half hoping it would be too strong for him to take his lesson. He would all but convince himself it *was* too strong—only to get there and hear Carlie say, "Okay, do your walk-around and we'll get started."

He smiled at the memory because he remembered, too, that once he was in the plane and had the engine going, his fears always evaporated. "Want to tweak her nose for me?" he asked Skip.

Skip went forward to prop the engine.

"Rich—" Debbie followed him closer to the plane. "Do you think this is a good idea? I mean, couldn't Jiggs or Wilkey do it as well?"

"Either one could, and a lot better," he told her, "if they'd had any chance to check out in the Lakes. But I'm the only one who's done any flying in it."

"You haven't done much."

"Enough, I think. It's a sweet-handling ship. And anyway, this may be my last chance to fly as a single, as part of the show. I don't want to miss it."

She nodded and forced a smile. "All right, go land on—" Her voice broke, and her smile became a grimace. "Oh, *damn* it! Don't get hurt, Rich!"

He'd started to turn away, but this stopped him. He put his arms around her. He held her and said, "Hey . . . hey, come on now," feeling helpless.

"I—I'm sorry." She lifted her tear-stained face. "Go . . . fly the wings off that old . . . jug!"

He laughed at her, then kissed her.

"Hey, what's holding things up?" Skip called, peering around from the front of the plane. "Oops, sorry," he said, and disappeared again.

They both laughed. "Excuse me while I go fly this old jug," Rich said. He stepped up into the rear cockpit, settled into the cushions and called, "Switch on!"

The engine caught at the first pull.

As he taxied east on the runway, past the grandstands, he looked out at the wall of people and saw them applauding. He saw Tommy at the announcer's table, gesturing dramatically, and knew he was talking it up. Dozens of cameras, including the large, red-eyed box atop the television platform, followed his progress down the runway; and so much attention, focused for the first time just on him, made him shy. He had to force himself to wave back at the crowd.

At the end of the runway, he swung around to face west, the direction of take-off, and did a quick preflight: controls, instruments, fuel level, trim. He ran the engine up to 1,500 rpm and checked the magnetos. A final glance at the windsock beside the runway, then he palmed the fat, round throttle handle forward as far as it would go. The Great Lakes shook itself and lumbered ahead.

It pulled left a little from engine torque, and Rich countered with right rudder. The tail came up, and Rich held forward stick a few seconds longer, to build up speed—then swept the stick back to his lap, and sent the Lakes soaring steeply skyward in front of the grandstands. He held it in the precipitous climb as long as he dared, almost long enough to scare himself —a stall this near the ground would be disastrous—but the big Warner radial kept the propeller turning, gnawing air, and the wings bucked and fluttered but refused to stop lifting. When he glanced at his instruments he was at 300 feet and going up like an elevator.

My God, he thought—and mentally heard the answer to the old joke: "Y-e-e-s?"

He leveled off at 700 feet, did a slipping turn to start back toward the stands, and let the speed begin to build for the entry to an inside loop.

While lining up, he glanced at the grandstands and saw the peculiar whitewash effect of several thousand faces turned upward, watching him. It distracted his attention only an instant. Then, seeing that his reference points were well aligned and he was at the correct altitude, he brought the control stick back to begin his loop. Gravity pressed him down in his seat—gently at first, then harder, then—*too hard!* He pulled his head down to look at the airspeed indicator, and saw that he was going much too fast.

For a moment his mind froze. He sat there while the Great Lakes dragged its nose up through the horizon and began to climb to the top of the loop. This was wrong—*wrong*—because at this speed, he'd never be able to pull out after starting down the back side. He'd tear the wings off, or cause a high-speed stall and plunge straight into the ground. He tried to look at the airspeed indicator again, but there seemed to be a red haze in front of his eyes. . . . He relaxed.

The instant he relaxed, it seemed natural and obvious to put the stick forward, holding the Great Lakes at the vertical until the stall began. Then he came in with rudder and aileron. The result was that he performed the first really perfect vertical snap roll he'd ever flown—and it was almost as much fun as if he'd done it on purpose.

Obviously, the secret was to relax.

This was something he'd always known he should do, but never really experienced before. Now he did experience it, and felt something new and strange and pleasant begin to happen to him. As he angled down into a dive that brought the ground flashing toward him—holding it until the last possible moment before dragging the nose up and through in a long hawklike sweep—he felt himself growing wings.

He felt them take root and spread; they were the Great Lakes's wings, but they became his as well. He felt the strength of them in his bones and muscles, felt his nerves spin out through wood and wire and fabric until the painless pressure of wind-wrapped lift and power were his. . . .

And then he flew.

He flew all the maneuvers he knew: everything he'd studied so long under Carlie, and practiced over and again himself, and never *really* known how to fly till now. He was taught over again, and right, by a teacher with blue-striped wings and body, a jackhammer-voiced instructor that shouted its pleasure or dissatisfaction at him:

"*Thus*, we fly the square loop, with full power to the vertical (balance with the rudder!), then over onto our back, easing up on power. Now, throttle off, over and down with opposite rudder; hold it hard in the pullout, and come back in with throttle—fine!

"Regular loops? No problem. . . . Rolls? They're easy. . . . Stalls? Do them any way you like, and when you've done them, free the controls and we'll fly out. (This close to the ground, you'd better help, though.) One maneuver leads to the next—naturally, normally, with the grace and rhythm of flight; that *is* flight—all you need do is:

"LOOK. Look well ahead, for that's where you'll be in the next fraction of a second, in the time it takes you to react.

"LISTEN. Listen to my engine, and the sound of my propeller, and the whispered vibrations all through my body. These tell you what I am doing, what I'm about to do, and how much I can do.

"FEEL. Feel the weight of gravity, the tug of centrifugal force in turns, the power of the wind's lift across our wings. The air is a clumsy giant, capable of supporting a jet liner or dropping a bird—but its power is unlimited for those who know how to use it."

The Great Lakes whispered and purred and roared at him in his own voice:

"Inverted flight? It's simple, really. Speed 120 mph,

stick over, and keep the nose straight with rudder while we half-roll. *There.* Now, forward stick to keep the nose on the horizon, and a plane flies the same except that up and down are reversed. Simple. Carlie wanted a few low passes to show us off? Very well, we'll give them a couple. Inverted."

He circled east and began to descend; he waited until the right border of the runway was aligned perfectly with his nose spinner, and then half-rolled. Correcting for drift, he came on down through 100 feet, added some power, and shoved the stick a little farther forward to stop his sink. It took several minor adjustments to establish perfect, level flight, and by the time he did the grandstands were going by on his right. Throttle back to full, he climbed to 200 feet and rolled back to straight-and-level.

He'd done it! He'd flown low-level inverted, and it hadn't been all that hard really. His palms were wet but that was normal, and he wiped them on his knees as he circled back to the stands. Passing them, he reached over the side of the plane to point.

He pointed at the aluminum poles and red, crepe-paper streamer used for the ribbon pick-up.

Flying out east of the field, now, he wondered where this idea had come from. It might not be such a good one, actually. A fly-by at 100 feet was one thing, but those poles were only thirty feet high—less than one third the ground clearance. Suddenly, it seemed a very questionable idea indeed, and he considered calling it off. No, better yet, he would make one pass at it, flying safely above the ground, and then he'd land.

That would hold the fans' interest and fill a little more time.

Lining up his target, he rolled the Great Lakes over once again.

As he looked forward across the stubby, rounded engine cowling, he saw the infield and landing strip and grandstands, upside down on his right. Using the near edge of the runway for a guide, he let the plane sink a little lower. Not *too* low, he remembered.

Tommy would get the most out of the situation. He'd explain to the crowd how Rich had never flown this stunt before—tell them it was a trial run, or something—so they wouldn't expect too much. Tommy would know what to say.

When he saw the runway numbers float by beneath him—over his head, actually—he realized he'd already descended a little lower than he'd intended.

That was all right; a touch of throttle would stop the sink. More would lift him up and away from that flat, hard, unyielding surface; away from the gray-green carpet that unreeled below his head; would carry him— *Had the engine missed a beat?*

No. No, it was his imagination. The tendency every pilot has to hear odd noises whenever the proper function of the engine is vital. What's referred to jokingly as "automatic rough."

But the engine was all right, and the plane flew straight on—on, toward the slender metal poles that reached up like skeleton fingers. Rich watched the miniature men who held the poles grow larger. They were upside-down men, standing on an earth that rocked and tilted, as though hinged to the horizon; and Rich had an overpowering urge to shove the throttle full ahead, to climb away and thus avoid the reaching metal fingers. Another second . . . two seconds . . . three—and he could almost hear the pistol-shot report of one of the poles striking his wing, sawing through wood and fabric. The shearing of frail framework and flimsy covering that would send him twisting, turning, diving into the ground like a gut-shot bird.

One second more he sat frozen, and stabbed the throttle—and knew he was too late.

The airplane shuddered as the engine coughed, then roared. A vibration passed over the plane's body like the shadow of a cloud. The Great Lakes climbed steeply, ponderously, almost ready to stall, until it reached 400 feet and then Rich compelled his muscles to untense and let the nose down slightly. He gained enough speed to roll the ship right side up again.

For a while longer he sat very still, expecting something to happen. He knew he'd flown too close—far, far too close. He hadn't meant to fly that close, but had done it anyhow, and now— He caught sight of something fluttering, out the corner of one eye. *Something on the wing!* His heart nearly choked him before he was able to turn his head and see what was wrong. And when he did, he gasped with surprise and felt like laughing and crying, both.

Twisted through the wing wires, blowing back from them, and snapping free in the wind, was a long strip of red crepe paper. He'd caught the ribbon.

Chapter 14

He brought the plane in and landed it. He saw people waving to him from the announcer's stand, so he angled the Great Lakes to the side of the runway and braked it to a halt. Instants later, friends, show officials, and spectators had surrounded the plane.

Skip Scott hopped onto the Lakes' wing root and reached into the cockpit to thump Rich on the back and shoulders. "Beautiful!" he shouted. "Just beautiful! When the heck did you learn to do the ribbon pick-up?"

"Just now," he said—and took advantage of Skip's surprise to climb out of the cockpit past him.

Maurice and Jiggs were waiting to greet him as he stepped to the ground. *"Epetant, mon vieux!"* one cried, while the other scowled with mock ferocity and muttered, *"Dummkopf!"* Each shook hands with him, and Rich laughed with them, ignoring the watery feeling in his knees. "Would you guys do me a favor? Take the Lakes down to the hangar for me? It could get damaged with this mob around."

"Sure thing," Jiggs said and, with Skip and Maurice

helping, began to wheel the airplane away. Rich turned toward the announcer's table, but didn't get far. He found himself face to face with a stormy-looking Tommy Tomkins.

"All right, young fella, I want a word with you!"

"Oh, hi, Tommy."

" 'Hi,' he says!" He turned to Debbie, who was with him. "I tell him to go out and do a few, simple book maneuvers, and what happens? Next thing I know, he's doing his best to get plastered all over the landscape!"

"I was only—" Rich tried to put in.

"Of course I realize that's just a beginning. First solo performance. Next time, I guess maybe you could try something fancy—like flying through a brick wall, for instance. Or maybe get yourself shot out of a cannon and land in the cockpit, or even—"

"Dad, stop!" Debbie said, putting herself between the two men. "He was marvelous and you know it, you even said so on the public address."

"Well, I had to say something."

"Maybe, but you didn't have to go quite that far. Calling him the best young aerobat in the Western Hemisphere."

Tommy reddened. "You got to exaggerate a little. Just talkin' it up, was all."

Rich said, "I really am sorry if I gave you a scare. I hadn't planned on getting quite that low."

Tommy seemed slightly mollified. "Well . . . actually, it wasn't too bad a job. Pretty good, in fact.

In fact—" He checked himself and said, "But all the same, it was a darn-fool thing to do!"

"I know," Rich said.

"Mr. Newman?" someone called. They saw a man in shirtsleeves, wearing a headset, followed by another who was carrying a shoulder-mounted TV camera. Pushing toward them through the crowd, the first man said, "Hold it a minute, we'd like to get a few words with you. *Give us some room here!* No, you stay," he advised Tommy. "*Okay on camera?* Yeah, here he is now. . . ."

Deke Barrett shouldered through the crowd to join them.

The TV announcer was elegantly dressed, wearing a white tie with a colored shirt, and a rich-fabricked sportscoat that was much too hot for the July weather. Sweat stood out in beads along Deke Barrett's hairline and around the edges of his makeup. He was carrying a hand-held microphone and talking into it as he walked: ". . . where we'll be chatting with the young man who just gave us all such a big thrill, and here he is—if we can get through, please, thank you—here he is now, Rich Newman. Rich, can we talk to you a minute? How are you feeling after that great performance, Richie?"

"Fine, thanks."

"Wonderful. And I want to say that was terrific, a great job. It's hard to believe, but we understand it's the first time you've done that ribbon pick-up stunt in public. Is that right?"

"Yes," he said, conscious of the flattery. "That's right."

"Sensational! Pretty risky too, I'd guess, especially the first time."

"There's some," he admitted, thinking Barrett meant risk to the pilot.

"God forbid," the sportscaster continued, "that anything should go wrong—but if it did, with a huge crowd like this on hand, a lot of people could get hurt, couldn't they?"

"Well, that's not likely," he said. He was about to mention some of the precautions taken to safeguard the audience—but Barrett didn't give him the chance.

"But it is possible, right? People could be injured if a plane went out of control, isn't that correct?"

"It's possible, but—"

"But I suppose we just have to hope nothing like that happens. Tell us something else, Richie. The word's been going around that you might be leaving the Tomkins Air Show in the near future. Would you care to comment?"

Tommy had been standing, waiting, not paying too much attention to the conversation. He looked at Deke now, startled, and then at Rich.

"No, I—I'd rather not," Rich stammered.

"According to the rumor, you'll be going with Tri-Cities Airways."

He realized the information must have come from Jocelyn. He wondered if she could have realized how much it would hurt and embarrass him to have it made public this way. If only he'd had a chance to talk to Tommy first. "I told you, I'd rather not—"

Tommy turned suddenly and strode away.

Rich made a move to follow, but felt Deke take hold of his arm, and heard him say, "Well then, we don't want to press you, do we?"

An angry answer occurred to him, but before he could give it, Deke continued:

"Tell us this, though. The old-fashioned air shows are on the way out, aren't they? I mean, they were all right in their day, but in an age of space travel they seem pretty out of date, wouldn't you say?"

Rich had stopped trying to pull away from the man. "What?"

"These antiques you fly aren't too exciting in an age of supersonic jets and rockets to the moon. People are losing interest in them, don't you think?"

He decided he'd taken all he was going to. "No. I'll tell you what I think. I think you don't know what you're talking about—rockets, jets, *or* antique planes."

Deke Barrett looked startled, then recovered. "I see. Well, now—" he chuckled good-naturedly, "you could be right, I guess."

"So I'll tell you about them."

The man discovered that now it was Rich who gripped him by the arm. All he could do was stand and listen:

"The trouble with people like you, Mr. Barrett, is that for a thing to be any good, it has to be modern and expensive. An old biplane won't qualify, obviously, because it's not big enough or fast enough for you. It doesn't even occur to you that there could be anything fine or beautiful about an old ship—you've never seen them advertised, so they can't be worth much."

"Now just a—"

"Well, this may come as a big surprise to you, but airplanes weren't invented just to watch movies on. As a matter of fact, I don't think the Wright brothers were even very interested in *going* anywhere. They just wanted to fly, and a lot of people in this business know how they felt, because we love to fly too. That's really all an air show is about.

"But you're right, I suppose, when you say shows like ours are on their way out. Most are gone already. The planes are getting too old, and even if new ones were built, there aren't many pilots left who'd care to fly them. So maybe the shows will be gone soon. I don't suppose people like you will miss them.

"Some people will, though. People will miss them who can remember when flying was a challenge and the sky was a new frontier. Some others who actually took part will remember that, at the controls of an old biplane, you could find out how good a man you were. That sort of thing doesn't interest people who don't want to know, of course. I'll tell you something. Just being a small, unimportant part of the Tomkins Air Show has been the most wonderful experience of my life. And I can only pity anyone who hasn't got the brains or the imagination to understand why it was."

He released Deke Barrett's arm, and without waiting

for the man to recover long enough to frame an answer, he turned and walked away.

He pushed through the crowd, toward the public-address announcer's table, looking for Tommy. He had to find the man now, and explain about Jake Svanne, the job offer, why he'd decided to accept it. He only wished he understood it all a little better himself. When he reached the table, Tommy wasn't there, his place having been taken by the Air Force captain who announced for the Blue Angels.

He looked at the people around the table, but could not spot Tommy among them. He was about to start asking if anyone had seen him when he heard Debbie calling.

"Rich—over here!"

She was behind him, coming from the direction of the main gate. He went to meet her. "Hi, where's Tommy?" he asked.

"He went back to the motel." She sounded out of breath. "He asked Captain Henning to do the sign-off for him after the Angels are through, and then he left."

"Okay," he said, and started past her.

"Where are you going?"

"To talk to him."

"Rich, don't."

He looked questioningly at her.

"I—I tried to get him to wait," she said, "but he wouldn't. He's upset. He'll get over it, and I know he only wants what's best for you, but it was a shock finding out that way."

Rich swore under his breath.

"It'll be all right," she told him. "Just give him a little time."

"That's what I was doing—and look how it worked out. It won't help to wait any longer."

"At least let me talk to him first." When Rich started to shake his head, she touched his arm and hurried on: "Please. I won't try to speak for you, or explain, I'll just make sure he's ready to listen. I think it's important."

"Well. . . ."

"Where are you going to be, later?"

"In my room, I guess. I'll go back and wait, as soon as I've finished taking care of the Lakes."

"Good. I'll call you there." She pressed his arm, then turned and hurried away.

Several people stopped him to offer congratulations as he walked down to Hangar Four. A few youngsters asked for his autograph. By the time he reached the hangar, the Blue Angels were concluding their performance and the Air Force captain was winding up the show. He mentioned all the performers, thanking them, and though Rich heard his own name spoken and the applause following it, this gave him little pleasure. In a way it was painful, since he knew all that was over for him, now. Finished.

He found the main doors closed, and so went in at the side entrance and made his way through a sort of machine-shop area, abandoned for the weekend, to the floor space where the planes were parked. The

Great Lakes was where Jiggs and Skip had put it, in a clearing near the main doors. It stood just where rays of sun fell from a window on the west wall, bathing it in late-afternoon light. It looked like the star of the show, getting ready to bow.

Rich gazed at it a moment, lost in admiration, then remembered why he'd come. He went and found some clean rags, and set to work. He wiped down the belly and the undersides of the bottom wings, removing all the oil sprayed or spilled during inverted flight, working his way back toward the tail. He took his time, enjoying the labor; when he reached the rear of the airplane, he lay on his back and slid under the stabilizer and elevator. He was there when he heard footsteps on the hangar floor.

The footsteps approached and stopped, and when he turned his head he could see a man's shoes a few feet away from him. Curious, he wormed out from under the plane. "Oh . . . hello," he said to Jake Svanne.

The older man stood with his fists on his hips and looked first at the plane, then at Rich, then shook his head slowly. "That wasn't in our agreement, you know," he said.

He understood. "No, I guess it wasn't."

"We agreed on Carlie Hatcher. I never intended for some green kid to practice low-level flying in it."

He got to his feet, stung by this reference to himself. "It so happens Carlie couldn't fly today. He was sick."

"I know all about it," Jake said, "and that doesn't

excuse or explain anything. There are a couple of other pilots who could have done the job—fellows with a little more experience than you've got."

"Nobody else was checked out in the Lakes, though."

"Checked out? I suppose you were checked out to fly that ribbon pick-up routine."

"Well, I. . . ."

"You weren't, of course. The truth is, Jiggs or Wilkey could have done what you were *supposed* to do. Without being checked out. The one stunt that neither of them would have attempted in an unfamiliar plane, without practice, was the one *you* hadn't practiced either. Right?"

He hesitated, then nodded.

"Right," Jake Svanne said. "And now that that's straight, maybe you'll tell me something else. Why'd you do it? What the devil even made you try?"

Rich smiled ruefully, and said, "I've been asking myself the same question ever since it happened."

"Do you have any answers?"

"I'm not sure. I'm not sure my answers would make sense to anyone else."

Jake Svanne sat down on the base of the Great Lakes' wing and braced his hands on his knees. "Try me."

He drew a breath and rubbed his jaw with one hand, thinking. "It just seemed like my last chance, I guess. I've dreamed for so long about being part of the show—getting good enough to fly a real routine—when this happened today, it was like something saying, Okay, now or never. I didn't plan to do it. When

I took off, I just meant to fly my series from the opener
and a few other things, I wasn't sure what. Then everything felt so good, I didn't want to stop. I just wanted
to keep on until I'd flown it all. I wanted to get everything in, and after I'd done all the rest, it seemed
as though I had to do that too." He fell silent. A moment
later he looked at Jake Svanne—but the hangar was
growing dark now, and he couldn't see the man's eyes.

"And now?" Svanne said after a short silence.

"Now?"

"Do you *still* not want to stop? Would you prefer
to go on with stunt-flying? Do you want to cancel our
deal, in other words?"

"That's not what I said—"

He didn't get to finish. Someone switched the light
on in the hangar. It had been getting rather dark and
the sudden brilliance was blinding. It was hard to iden-
tify the two people standing near the office entrance
at first, then Rich heard a man's voice say:

"Go on, son, tell him if you want."

It was Tommy Tomkins. Debbie was with him.
Rich groaned inwardly; all he needed now, he thought,
was to get caught between Jake and Tommy; between
his new employer and one of his best friends.

"You may be used to sticking to your deals," Tommy
said, coming nearer, "but not everyone operates that
way. That's something you have to learn, Rich—some
folks back out on bargains without giving it a second
thought."

Tommy hadn't so much as looked at the other man

yet, but Jake Svanne sighed and said, "Good evening, Thomas. Nice seeing you."

Tommy still ignored him. "Well, sorry if I broke in on you, Rich. Debbie said you wanted to talk, and I thought we might find you here. We can do it later. Just remember, though, you can change your mind. You're always welcome to come back to the show."

Rich nodded. He wanted to say something, but mere thanks wasn't enough, and he couldn't think what was.

Jake broke the silence. "Since you're here, Thomas—" he began.

"I was just leaving."

"Oh, that's too bad. I'd wanted to talk some business with you."

Tommy stopped and turned to look straight at the man for the first time. "You wanted to talk business? With *me*?"

"That's right."

"Well, now," Tommy said slowly, "I'd like to do that, but I'm afraid I forgot to bring my snakebite kit with me, and—"

"Dad!" Debbie said.

But Jake Svanne had burst out laughing. He shook his head after a moment and said, "Okay, Thomas, maybe I deserve that. I'd still like to tell you what I have in mind. I think you might be interested."

"Well, I don't."

"Don't you? Or are you afraid you might be?" When Tommy hesitated, Jake grinned. "Can't hurt to listen, can it?"

Tommy snorted, but made no move to go.

The other man's expression grew serious. "I'll tell you how it is. Some things I saw, watching television earlier today, got me to thinking. Gave me some ideas, too. For one thing, it occurred to me that this—" he nodded at the Great Lakes "—was a pretty good piece of advertising. A lot of people saw that Tri-Cities emblem today, and it hardly cost me a thing."

"What do you mean 'hardly?'" Tommy couldn't resist saying.

Jake spread his hands and shrugged. He looked at Rich, then. "Something else I enjoyed was the way you stood up to that nitwit, Barrett. You made a lot of sense. Some things you said about the old-time planes, and about flying itself . . . well, those are things I once believed in. Still do, now that I think about it. So that's another reason for wanting to offer you a little business proposition," he said, turning back to Tommy.

"Here it comes," the other said. "Get the women and children off the street."

"All right, damn it!" Jake said, getting up and looking angry now. "If that's all you can think about—something that happened almost thirty years ago—we'll talk about that. What would you like, an apology?"

"No."

"That's good, because you aren't getting one. Look. I'm not especially proud of what I did, back then, but I'm not ashamed, either. It looks to me like we both got what we wanted. I got going in business,

and made a lot of money, which was what I wanted . . . you and Dorothea got married, and kept the
show, which was what both of you wanted. I'm not
all that sure who got the best of the deal," he added,
turning and walking away a few steps.

Tommy said nothing, but he put his arm around
Debbie and drew her closer.

When Jake turned back, he saw them standing
together, and nodded slightly. "My offer has to do
with the Lakes. If you're interested, I'd like you to
keep it in the show, Thomas. It was built for that
kind of work, and I hardly ever use it. It would make
sense to get some publicity value from it—and might
solve some of your problems at the same time."

"Yes, it would."

"In that case, I'd expect the plane to carry the TCA
emblem, and for it to be mentioned on the public-
address system occasionally. At least once during each
show, say. In return, I pay all expenses for the aircraft,
maintenance, insurance, and so on. Does that sound
fair?"

"Fair?" Tommy repeated, his jaw a bit slack.

Debbie said, "It sounds almost too generous, Mr.
Svanne."

"Well, it isn't. The TV coverage alone will be more
than worth it. In fact, I'd even like to take care of
my pilot's salary when he flies for you."

"Your pilot?" Tommy said, on his guard again.

"This one," Jake said, nodding at Rich. "I thought
you knew he was working for me, now."

There was an instant of stunned silence—then Debbie turned and threw herself into Rich's arms with a delighted squeal. "Oh, *Richie!*" she cried.

Tommy looked at them in surprise, then began to smile.

Jake Svanne cleared his throat. "Naturally, you'll want all this in writing."

"All what?"

"Our agreement—what I'm paying, in return for what I'm getting. Assuming we have a deal, that is."

"I think we may be able to work something out," Tommy said. "Why don't we go back to my place and iron out the details?"

They began walking toward the hangar door.

"Good idea," Jake said. "This time, we want to make sure everybody will be happy, right?"

Tommy opened the door for the other man, then paused a moment to glance over his shoulder. "I think everybody's going to be," he said.

It was a while before Rich and Debbie realized they were alone.